DREAMCATCHER

DREAMCATCHER

Sheila Spencer-Smith

CHIVERS

British Library Cataloguing in Publication Data available

This Large Print edition published by BBC Audiobooks Ltd, Bath, 2009.
Published by arrangement with the author.

U.K. Hardcover ISBN 978 1 408 43276 1
U.K. Softcover ISBN 978 1 408 4 3277 8

Printed and bound in Great Britain by
CPI Antony Rowe, Chippenham and Eastbourne

A BAD START

Maria hit the brake pedal and screeched to a halt in the narrow street, narrowly avoiding hitting the oncoming car. The other driver leapt out of his vehicle and came striding towards her . . . tall, long-legged, blond hair, jeans. And an angry expression that would do justice to a man-eating tiger. Or woman-eating.

But he was equally at fault, she reminded herself as she got out to confront him.

'What do you think you're doing?' he demanded.

'Just driving with extreme care. Unlike you.'

He gave a short laugh. 'Driving carefully in the wrong direction down a one-way street? No-one could accuse me of that.'

She glanced at him in dismay. 'The wrong way? I . . . I hadn't noticed.'

'Obviously not.'

'An honest mistake,' she said.

'If you say so.'

Their cars were bonnet to bonnet with barely any space between them.

She pushed back her hair from her face with trembling hands.

'I'll reverse,' she said, mustering what little dignity she had left.

'No, I will.' He looked at her Fiesta and

then back at her as if he thought her capabilities were nil.

'No way,' Maria said. 'I'm in the wrong, as you pointed out. It's up to me to get out of your way.'

'I'm late for an appointment,' he said.

'Then we won't stand here passing the time of day.'

For an instant a smile seemed to reach his eyes before his glowering expression returned.

'Yes, well . . .' he began but she didn't wait to hear more.

No need to panic, she thought. She would just get on and do it and forget he was watching her every move. Fortunately she hadn't far to reverse before she was back on the main road. He edged along after her but had to wait his turn to filter into the traffic.

She pulled into the side of the road and once he'd disappeared into the distance she sat for a while with her head resting on the steering wheel, letting her thumping heartbeats subside.

Not a good start to the holiday. But no harm had been done and she was very close to Yarnley Wharf. Her sister's exuberant greeting would be like balm and her brother-in-law, Neil, would be pleased to see her, too, grateful that she could be with them to help crew the narrowboat that would be home to them for the next two weeks.

At last she raised her head and took a deep restorative breath. She put the car into gear and drove off. It didn't take her more than a few minutes to reach the entrance to the wharf and she quickly parked in the designated parking area.

As she opened the door and got out she looked round her with pleasure. Sunlight flickered on the rippling water between the boats tied up to the metal jetties. There was a cobbled quayside and attractive old buildings.

Polly and Neil obviously hadn't arrived yet so there was time to take a look around. Maria fumbled in her bag for the copy of the instruction sheet Polly had sent her in case she arrived first.

Dreamcatcher was the name of the boat she was looking for. The three of them were in for a wonderful time, drifting along past banks of wild iris and mooring beneath overhanging branches of willow trees as the mood took them. An idyllic existence far from the turmoil of normal daily life. She was really looking forward to it.

*   *   *

With mounting excitement she saw *Dreamcatcher* at the end of the row of narrowboats, immaculate with its green paint and brass fittings.

'Can I help you?' said a familiar voice behind her.

She hadn't expected ever to see him again and she spun round in consternation.

He wasn't glowering at her now but he still seemed unfriendly.

'You!' she said. 'You're in charge here?'

Silly question. Of course he was. Why else would he be holding a clipboard and looking as if he meant business?

'For the time being, yes.'

'I'm meeting someone,' she said.

'You're booked in for a narrowboat holiday?' He sounded annoyed, as if she had no business to be there.

Surely she'd come to the right place?'

'This *is* Yarnley Marina, isn't it?' she asked.

'And you are?' An expression of deep suspicion flickered across his face.

'Our booking is for Rankin,' she said. 'Our boat's name is *Dreamcatcher.* I can see it over there.'

Frowning, he glanced down at the clipboard and then at the narrowboat she had indicated. She had the distinct impression that something was wrong.

'And you're a member of the Rankin party?'

She nodded. 'That's my brother-in-law and sister.'

She looked anxiously towards the gate. Where were Polly and Neil? She was used to her dreamy brother-in-law taking his time but not her dynamic sister, Polly, who was always eager to be early for everything. And this trip was so important to them.

'One moment, please,' he ordered. 'Wait here.'

She watched him cross the cobbles to the office and vanish inside. There were sounds of raised voices and something being banged down on a hard surface. Feeling awkward, she moved closer to *Dreamcatcher* so as to be out of earshot.

He returned, frowning. 'I hope the rest of your party will be here soon for the briefing. I've another appointment at three. I can't miss it.'

'I'm Maria Howard. Can't you just tell me whatever we need to know?'

'No way. Rules.' He checked his board again. 'Howard you said?'

She nodded.

'There's no Howard down on the crew list.'

'That's because the plans were changed at the last minute. I'm stepping in for someone who couldn't make it.'

He shot her a distrustful look. 'It's a condition of hire that everyone is named on the contract. I take it you have some means of identification?'

Surely he wasn't expecting her to come equipped with a passport? She imagined handing it to him and watching him examine the photo that made her look like some sort of zombie who had just had an electric shock.

'Driving licence?' he suggested.

'Packed in the bottom of my bag back in the car. The others will vouch for me when they get here. They must have been held up.'

She looked round hopefully. Where were they?

'You can't take the boat out until you've all had your briefing, and if you miss your slot you'll have to wait until the next free appointment,' he said. 'They're cutting it fine.'

They were indeed. 'Well, I don't know what the arrangements are,' she said. 'All I know is that my sister and brother-in-law asked me to help them out by crewing for them. I came prepared with all my kit and everything.'

He raised a quizzical eyebrow. 'And those shoes?'

She looked down at her feet. 'What's wrong with them?'

'Show me the soles.'

She raised one foot.

He snorted with derision. 'You need non-slip shoes,' he said. 'The shop in town sells suitable ones.'

She looked back at him in defiance. Why did she get the feeling he didn't want her here . . . or Polly and Neil for that matter?

'I'm sure the others'll be here soon,' she said.

He glanced at his watch, frowning. 'I'll give

6

them half an hour.'

'They'll have arrived by then,' said Maria.

He turned away from her and headed back towards the office. 'Give me a shout when they come,' he called over his shoulder. 'You know where I am.'

There was a café tucked away in a corner of the wharf with wooden tables set out on the cobbles outside. She needed a coffee and from there she could keep watch for Polly and Neil.

Inside, a long bar at one end did service as the counter. Maria placed her order and then turned to look at the paintings that covered each wall. They were local scenes mostly, of the canal and old stone bridges, reflections of trees in water, several locks including a staircase of five or more, the entrance to a tunnel and even one painted inside a tunnel with light showing at the end. Not one was painted in a traditional way though. The artist, Lucas Slane, must have enjoyed himself slapping colour about in this uninhibited way.

Maria smiled as she stepped back for a better view. The force of emotion shining from each of them surprised her. Extraordinary. She went forward again and the clarity fused into vivid colours that shouted at the eye. How had the artist known of the effect from far off? Thoughtfully she tried to work it out. Experience, she supposed.

Now, feeling more relaxed after her earlier tension, she carried her drink and salad sandwich outside to one of the wooden tables. Dazzling sunshine glinted on the roofs of the old buildings on the other side of the canal basin. Some had been lovingly restored and were now apartments with balconies overlooking the cobbled quayside.

Maria watched as a group of people appeared and headed towards one of the narrowboats and clambered aboard. One of them, a young girl, released the rope attached to a ring on the jetty, the engine sprang to life and they began to move off. The cheerful atmosphere pleased Maria. She was glad about the promised tuition Polly had told her about. It was good to know that they wouldn't be totally ignorant landlubbers as they set off on their maiden voyage. If Mr Jobsworth in the office allowed them to, of course.

* * *

Maria had found herself being roped into the canal trip a week ago when, early one morning, her sister had phoned her with an urgent request. Polly's voice reached a crescendo as she gabbled about narrow-boats and get-away-from-it-all and brilliant opportunities.

By the time Maria had managed to make sense of what was being said she felt limp. She had never known her sister so excited.

'So you're inviting me to go on holiday with

you and Neil?'

'Insisting, Maria, insisting.'

'But why?'

'A thousand reasons.'

'Tell me one.'

'We need you, Maria, seriously. I'm not making it up. We won't be able to go if you don't come too.'

'Why not?'

'Because Neil's cousin has pulled out of the trip and we need at least two able-bodied adults to crew the boat. To work the locks, you see.'

'But why on earth are you and Neil going on a narrowboat holiday? I can't imagine it being your sort of thing. You usually head off to the sun, to Marbella or the Canary Islands?'

Polly giggled. 'I'll fill you in on the reasons later. Maria, my dear devoted sister, you won't let us down will you? Say you'll come.'

Put like that how could she have refused? Polly knew that Maria had two empty holiday weeks ahead of her since she'd split from Gary.

'All right, Polly, you're on,' she said.

'Wow, brilliant. You won't regret it I promise you.'

A thought struck her. 'Hang on a minute, Polly,' she said. 'Didn't you say you need two able-bodied adults? So . . . you and Neil, doesn't that make two?'

'Yes, but we've never done this sort of thing

9

before and a spare pair of hands won't go amiss. Anyway, it will be nice to spend some time with you and the break will do you good,' Polly went on persuasively.

Polly was right. An unexpected holiday was what she needed at this present moment in her life. Action, plans to be made and carried out. Things to think about. Like what to pack.

In the end she'd settled for shorts and sleeveless tops, a couple of thick jerseys and her oldest jeans. On impulse she'd added her favourite flowery top and new jeans and strappy sandals in case they found themselves at a smart canal-side restaurant.

The long dress she'd been saving for Gary's firm's next social function?

No, not for this.

*   *   *

Now, Maria gazed out across the canal and thought about Gary. She still missed him a lot. Of course you'd miss someone . . . anyone . . . who you'd spent a lot of time with.

But almost with shame she remembered her quick stab of relief when Gary had walked away to leave her sitting at a riverside restaurant table, alone. The feeling had lasted a mere second but it had been there. How could that be when it was obvious he was walking out of her life for ever?

And yet, if she was totally honest, things

hadn't been good between them for some time. Goodness knows she'd tried hard enough but in the end she'd had to admit that the magic had gone out of their relationship. Once or twice she'd even been on the brink of finishing the relationship herself. Now Gary had done it for her.

They had gone down to their favourite place on the Thames and Gary had chosen a table outside in the shade of a spreading willow. After they had eaten he had looked troubled, awkward, and then all his worries and regrets about their deteriorating relationship had come spilling out. They had no future together, Gary said. Better to find out now than later.

Of course it was. Nothing was more sensible than that.

He had gazed at her unhappily when eventually he got up to leave, and she hadn't tried to stop him. She knew that when he got together with his mates he would forget her at once. That was Gary. Living for the moment and enjoying life as it came. It was what had attracted her to him in the first place, his ability to slough off all his worries and live only for the present moment. Probably he'd lined up a new holiday companion already.

She'd watched him get into his car and drive away and felt nothing.

So it had been a surprise to Maria to discover how lonely she'd felt, how much she'd missed Gary's company. But not any more. Oh no. No more moping about the place, thanks to Polly. What better way to get over a broken relationship than to take part in an activity completely new to her?

* * *

Now, Maria tucked a loose strand of hair behind her ear and finished her coffee. Her decision to come narrowboating had pleased Polly and that was something. She herself could forget the plans that she and Gary had had for this fortnight—although ironically they'd intended to go sailing.

Then she heard familiar voices. Polly and Neil at last. The man in the office had heard them arriving too and appeared with his clipboard.

They came rushing up, laden with several bags. And now there was a flurry of activity with Polly's voice raised in consternation.

'What a nuisance!' she said rushing up to Maria, her face woebegone. 'This man refuses to let us on board.'

'Not for another hour at least,' he said firmly.

Neil looked resigned to the wait but Polly was a different matter.

'No way!' Her face reddened as she stepped towards him. 'The traffic was bad on the motorway. Not our fault! I insist we go aboard at once.'

'Polly, please . . .' Maria began. 'He's got an appointment at three. It's not his fault you're late either.'

ALL HANDS ON DECK!

Polly, fuming, was pacified at last by Neil's suggestion they should go for a meal. Leaving their assortment of bags with Maria's inside the office, they wandered along the road from the wharf and found a small café where they could get fish and chips.

This took up quite a bit of time and when they had finished, Maria slipped into the shoe shop next door and equipped herself with new trainers. She dumped her old ones in the nearest waste bin, still smarting a little at the sensible advice she had been given about slippery soles.

They wandered back to the wharf and Neil strolled off a little way along the towpath by himself, deep in thought. As the girls lingered by the office, Polly explained to Maria why this holiday was so important to them.

'You see, Neil's cousin, Steve, has been offered the chance to buy into a narrowboat hiring company. And now that Neil's been made redundant from his accountancy firm, I think it would be a wonderful opportunity for us to invest his redundancy money and go in with Steve.'

'A narrowboat business?' said Maria. 'That's a big change.' This was the last thing she'd expected to hear but Polly was always full of surprises.

'It's always been Steve's dream you see,' Polly went on. 'He's been planning it for years, so he wants to make sure we really are committed to the business and can cope with the boats. And he's a hard taskmaster.'

'I see,' Maria said, though she wasn't too sure she did.

'Steve insists we have time on the water to see what's involved with narrowboats. And since one from this wharf needs to be delivered to Bemerton Marina he decided we should do it. That chap from the office has probably checked all that out by now.'

'And it won't matter my name not appearing on his list?'

Polly shook her head. 'He can phone Steve to check if there's a problem. We've got nearly two weeks to get the boat there. A sort of test you see. Sink or swim.'

'Neither, I hope,' said Maria, who wasn't even sure where Bemerton was.

'Steve says another hiring company is itching to take over the business that he's interested in and we're going to stop that for all our sakes. Sadly, Steve's mother-in-law's seriously ill in New Zealand so he and his wife

14

have flown there to visit her. That's why we asked you to stand in for him, Maria. Between us we can get the boat to Bemerton. That's all we have to do and we're accepted.'

'I hope I won't let you down.'

'Of course you won't. You've always liked all these outdoor sporty things like sailing . . .' Polly broke off, confused. 'Me and my big mouth.'

Maria patted her hand and hastened to reassure her. 'It's all right, really it is, Polly. I'm OK.'

*   *   *

And standing here in this bright canal basin she felt she was. For the last hour or two she had forgotten Gary and the holiday sailing plans they had made together.

Polly smiled too. 'Steve is keen to have someone in the family come in with him but we must decide quickly. And we've got to get the boat to Bemerton by Friday week all in one piece. There'll be a lot for us to learn, of course, we'll need to know all about boat maintenance and things like that but that can wait until we know for sure that we're taking over the business.'

'What does Neil think about all this?'

Polly smiled. 'Think, Maria . . . a business of our own . . . or almost our own! But I've got to persuade Neil. You know what he's like. He's

15

dithering. We've got to work on him before it's too late.'

'Doesn't Neil get any say in the matter?'

Polly looked surprised. 'Of course not. It's for his own good.'

Maria glanced at the tall thin figure of her brother-in-law and felt a stab of sympathy. He stood on the canal bank, shoulders hunched, staring down into the water. She wasn't at all sure that Neil would like this sort of life but that was none of her business. She was here to help out and she would do her best.

And of course her sister had enough determination for the two of them. Polly was courageous, brave, willing to take chances. Now that Neil was out of a job it was a wonderful opportunity for them as she said . . . if it worked.

'Thanks for filling me in,' Maria said. 'I understand how important all this is for you. But why were you late getting here?'

'We stopped for supplies at a supermarket,' Polly said.

Maria nodded, imagining her sister's frustration in the long check-out queue.

'Look, Polly,' she said. 'I think the guy from the office is ready for us.'

*   *   *

The engine chugged in a satisfactory way as they moved out into the centre of the canal basin. Neil stood with his hand clenched on the tiller and the tip of his tongue protruding from his lips in concentration.

'I'm Luke,' the blond young man told them, flashing a smile at Polly.

She smiled back, her earlier irritation gone.

'Hi there, Luke,' she said. 'Are you coming some of the way with us?'

'Just to make sure you all feel fully confident handling *Dreamcatcher.*'

'Great,' she said. 'We'll soon learn with you to teach us won't we, Maria?'

He flicked a look at Maria and raised one eyebrow.

She shrugged. She wasn't won over by his good humour.

Why was he ladling on the charm when he had been so unfriendly earlier?

Polly, her dark eyes shining, was definitely smitten by his slow smile.

*   *   *

Slowly *Dreamcatcher* moved along the canal, and the tree-lined banks slid past as they rounded a bend. The towpath was well-trodden here and obviously used a lot. A couple of joggers passed them, and a man exercising his dog.

'Keep in the middle of the canal unless you're passing another boat and then move over to the right,' Luke told Neil, sounding

17

relaxed and confident. 'And for obvious reasons slow right down if the other boat's moored.'

They were moving at walking pace, passing the gardens of houses tucked away among trees. It was all so calm and peaceful, Maria thought, but perhaps that was because Luke was on board taking responsibility. When they were on their own it might be a different matter.

Luke looked at Polly. 'Your turn at the tiller now.'

'Me?' she croaked as she took over from Neil. But she soon began to relax. 'This is great,' she said happily.

She experimented a little to see what happened as she moved the tiller from side to side. The narrowboat was slow to respond.

'No need to be quite so fierce,' Luke said, smiling so warmly at her that Polly blushed.

Maria shot him a look of censure and Luke looked back at her, a bland expression on his face. She would give a lot to know his thoughts. He seemed to be setting himself out to charm deliberately.

When it was her turn to take over, Maria held the tiller firmly. She liked the feeling of being in charge. Rather daringly she turned up the speed a little.

They rounded another bend and now the scene was rural, still a few trees on one side of them but views on the other of open

18

countryside looking attractive in the late afternoon sunshine. Long grass and white cow parsley lined the towpath and yellow irises grew at the water's edge.

Peace and beauty, Maria thought. She could get used to this.

'This is where I leave you,' said Luke after a while. 'Bring her into the bank gently.'

Maria moved the tiller round, conscious of Luke's critical gaze.

'Go into neutral,' he shouted, too late.

They hit the bank with a thump.

Luke reached forward to move the lever and then took the tiller from her. 'Watch what I do,' he ordered. He manoeuvred the boat into the correct position so that bows and stern were close to the bank.

'Can you remember how to do that?' he asked, his tone icy.

She nodded. 'I'll do my best.'

'See you do.' He jumped off into the long grass and waved them on. 'Good luck.'

To Maria he didn't sound as if he really meant it. To her surprise he didn't look back as he set off swiftly along the towpath. She waited for a moment and then carefully moved the tiller so that *Dreamcatcher* moved away from the bank into the centre of the canal as if she had been doing this all her life.

'Well done, Maria,' said Polly. 'And now we're on our own.'

Her sister looked so happy that Maria

smiled too.

* * *

At last Polly suggested they moor for a rest and something to eat. Maria, still at the helm, pulled the tiller round, intending to bring the boat in gently this time. Too late she realised she had again come in at too sharp an angle and the nose of the boat was in danger of hitting the bank.

'Oh, Maria, watch out,' cried Polly, grabbing at the tiller.

Neil came up from below, looking worried as the two girls managed between them to shove the engine into reverse and to get themselves back on course with a roar and much churned up water.

'All part of life's rich tapestry,' said Polly laughing.

Maria laughed too though her hands were shaking. What an idiot. Still, they'd managed it and on their own and, with no critical person watching, it didn't matter too much. They had to learn, after all, and Luke was miles away by now.

She grabbed the central rope and jumped for the bank as they glided in.

'The mooring pegs,' she cried.

Neil found them and the hammer. He joined her on the bank and knocked both pegs into the ground, one at either end, and

20

attached the ropes.

'That's safe enough for now,' he said.

'Luke's not so bad is he?' said Polly, leaning back against the padded seat in the dining area and looked at Maria speculatively. 'In fact he's very much OK. A good-looker too. Don't you agree?'

'Stop it, Polly.'

'Aren't you even the tiniest bit interested?'

'Me? You're not serious?'

'All that floppy blond hair,' said Polly dreamily.

'And arrogance,' said Maria sharply.

Polly raised one eyebrow at her.

'No way.' Maria put the milk jug down on the table with more force than she intended.

'Oh well, he's probably spoken for, a gorgeous chap like that,' said Polly. 'Too bad he isn't on a narrowboat too and then we'd probably meet up with him every now and again.'

It was just as well they weren't likely to see him again, Maria thought, if this was the way Polly was going to carry on.

*   *   *

The light in the doorway darkened as Neil came down the steps to join them in the cabin. He straightened too soon and gave an exclamation as his head came in contact with the rim of the door.

He sat down quickly, rubbing his forehead. 'We'll have to watch that,' he said. 'I'm tired, I suppose. We all are. All that concentration takes it out of you.'

He was looking very pale, Maria couldn't help but notice.

Now, moored in this lovely spot eating the ham sandwiches Polly had prepared, they felt peaceful and secluded. With the engine silenced, birdsong filled the air. A pair of ducks headed past them, five ducklings in tow.

After they had eaten and cleared away, Neil found the map of the canal system and sat down beside Polly.

'We can't get through Leverton Locks till the morning,' he said. 'The lock keeper went off duty at five. Might as well stay here for the night, what do you girls say?'

Polly opened her mouth to disagree and then shut it again.

'Why not?' said Maria, yawning. 'We'll be fresh enough tomorrow to deal with anything.'

'OK then,' said Polly. 'But an early start. Bemerton, here we come!'

'And with plenty of time to get there,' Neil said, smiling. Then his face clouded. 'If all goes well of course.'

'And why shouldn't it?' said Polly, stretching.

Neil got up. 'I'll knock another mooring peg in.'

Later, as she lay in her narrow bed formed by the padded seats in the dining area, thoughts of Gary seeped unbidden into Maria's mind. Perhaps, in her exhaustion, being on the water reminded her of the sailing holiday plans that they'd made together and which she'd been looking forward to.

The medical practice where she'd worked as receptionist for the past five years had recently moved to new premises creating extra work for them all. She needed a holiday. And Gary was in the past . . .

She closed her eyes and willed sleep to come.

* * *

Next morning Maria woke to see the sun streaming through the windows on the towpath side. They'd been too tired last night to pull the curtains across since there was no one to see inside.

Remembering her sister's exhortations for an early start, she got out of bed and stretched. Then she looked at her watch. Six o'clock. She filled the kettle and while it was boiling opened the door to let in the morning air. The canal water looked like green silk reflecting the overhanging trees.

Groans greeted her when at last she

knocked at Polly and Neil's door and went into their cabin to wake them with mugs of steaming tea.

She drank her own sitting on the wooden seat by the tiller having first wiped off the beads of dew that glistened there. A moorhen paddled by, and then two tiny chicks, scattering the trees' reflections in their wake. Maria watched them until they were out of sight, feeling the soft glow of the early sunshine on her face.

She began to wonder if she'd imagined Luke's overly hostile reaction at the wharf yesterday. She frowned, remembering his expression of annoyed dismay on seeing her and learning of Polly and Neil's imminent arrival. So what did it mean? There seemed no good reason unless, of course, he had connections with the firm who were also anxious to take-over the business Polly and Neil were thinking of buying into.

*　　　*　　　*

Breakfast was postponed because Polly was so impatient to get going.

Soon they were approaching a stone bridge. Neil headed for the centre of the arch. By now they were moving so slowly the bump on the towpath side was minimal. Even so it was a shock.

Polly, down below, let out a shriek.

24

Neil bit his lip as he moved the lever forward a little. In the confined space they seemed to be moving very fast.

Once they'd passed safely beneath it, Maria looked back at the bridge. She could see that, because the towpath went under the bridge as well as the canal, they should have headed slightly to one side of centre. Should she mention that to Neil or keep quiet? She gave a little sigh, thinking that next time she might be the one having to steer clear of challenging obstacles. Her mouth felt suddenly dry.

In a rough nest among reeds lining the bank sat a bird too big to be a moorhen . . . Maria thought it must be a coot. They moved past gently and some petals from the overhanging hawthorn blossom drifted down like snow and lay on the water.

There were compensations for all the hassle. One of them was the chance to help Polly in a way that meant a lot to her. Hadn't she always said she owed her sister a big debt for bringing her up? Now she was doing something to help repay her for all those years of support. It was a good feeling.

WHAT IS LUKE UP TO?

As they approached the wide expanse of water that formed the basin at the entrance to the locks they saw that there were at least three other narrowboats there before them.

'That's good,' said Polly when she saw them. 'Gives us time to grab some food while we wait. I'll get the kettle on.'

She clattered down the steps in her unsuitable sandals and Maria smiled after her. You couldn't tell Polly anything, not even that she should be wearing non-slip flatties for her own safety. Lucky that Luke hadn't tried to advise Maria's volatile sister on suitable footwear or she might have pushed him into the canal instead of responding to his smiles with more of her own.

Maria jumped ashore with the mooring pegs as Neil brought them alongside the bank.

'I'd better go round and report to the lock keeper,' he said.

By the time he'd walked round on the towpath and crossed the bridge to get to the other side of the basin, Polly had their coffee ready.

'Some cereal?' she asked Maria. 'Come on, girl, get some food inside you. We've got great things ahead.'

'That lock entrance seems very narrow,' Maria observed as she carried her bowl and mug up to the well-deck.

'And here's Neil coming back now,' said Polly.

*   *   *

'Stop dallying about you two,' he called as he got within earshot. 'They're going to put us through first as we're new to it. Come with me, Polly, to work the lock gates. You can manage to get the boat over there on your own, can't you Maria?'

Could she? Maria emptied her coffee mug on to the bank as Neil disengaged the mooring ropes and threw them aboard.

'I'll try,' she said.

She waited until Neil's tall thin figure and her sister's shorter one, in white top and shorts, appeared on the wooden bridge over the lock gates.

Neil waved. This was it. Maria took a deep breath.

Ignoring the waving arms and shouts to hurry, she moved the narrowboat towards the opening. The lock gates closed behind her. Even now she dare not look up at Polly and Neil for fear of doing something stupid in this dank dark box.

A voice boomed, the lock keeper's. 'Keep her steady there, away from the gates.'

Maria looked up at the kindly face looking down at her. He was a big man, oozing confidence. He would tell her exactly what to do.

*   *   *

27

The water gradually rose and by the time she could look out over the walls to the shining countryside behind she felt a lot happier. Polly on one side of the lock gate and Neil on the other called out to her. Then they disappeared to go up to the next set of lock gates and get to work there while Maria waited for the signal from the lock keeper to move *Dreamcatcher.*

Then the same again and again. She began to lose count . . . was that four locks, or five?

And now she was in the final one with the lock keeper telling her that she would have to wait there because a boat was coming down and would go into the central pool first. Only then would *Dreamcatcher* be able to pass.

Neil joined her, looking slightly flushed. He took the central rope she threw to him and attached it to a handy bollard. Then he came aboard and sat beside her on the bench in the well-deck. The sun had caught the bridge of his nose.

'All right, Maria?'

She nodded.

'Good girl. You were brilliant. We may be waiting some time now. Polly's gone off to tell them what to do.'

Maria laughed. 'Are you enjoying this, Neil?'

'It has its moments,' he said. 'Better than I thought really. And you?'

'I'll tell you when we get to the top.'

He sighed. 'I'm not really sure it's for us in

28

the long term. But don't let that worry you, Maria. You're doing fine and we're getting the hang of things with the gates, Polly and me. Open the paddles first with the windlass, wait till the water comes up and then open the gates. It helps with two of us, one on each side. Ah, here she comes now.'

Polly looked the picture of health. She had caught the sun and her brown eyes sparkled. She threw herself down on the grassy bank and sat with her arms round her bare legs. 'You'll never guess who I saw up at the top? Luke, painting at an easel. He's going to join us for a coffee when we get out of here.'

Maria was horrified. 'Oh, Polly, I thought we had to get on?'

'Well, I'm starving. We didn't have much breakfast, remember?'

'We could eat on the move,' said Maria. Her sister's embarrassing plans to throw herself and Luke together had put paid to her appetite.

Polly scowled. 'What's the matter with you? After all this effort I want to rest for a bit, don't you, Neil?'

He looked from one to the other, obviously undecided how to placate both of them.

'Look, the other boat's coming out now,' said Maria.

They were on the move again. By the time she had manoeuvred *Dreamcatcher* past the other boat and into the bottom lock of the upper flight, Maria acknowledged to herself that Polly had a point about mooring for a rest. She felt incredibly tired.

*   *   *

It seemed to take a long time before *Dreamcatcher* was at last rising in the top lock and Maria could see the stretch of canal ahead of her. She also saw the figure that she knew to be Luke seated at an easel. He held his head slightly to one side as he scrutinised his work and seemed totally absorbed.

Concentrating hard, Maria drew alongside the bank. Polly caught the mooring rope and Maria passed the pegs and mallet to her.

As Maria sank down on the seat by the tiller she saw that her hands were trembling with relief that the staircase of locks was behind them. She hid both hands in the pockets of her shorts, embarrassed.

Luke put down his paintbrush and sauntered towards them.

'Hi, there,' he called. 'You managed that well, I hear?'

'Maria was brilliant,' Polly said with enthusiasm.

For a second, Maria's eyes met his, and his expression was inscrutable. Then he smiled. Maybe he thought her sister was covering up for her to hide her ineptitude. But she wouldn't be patronised.

30

Hastily she went down into the galley to put the kettle on and root out the tin of biscuits. Polly had invited him, so she could entertain him. She herself would keep out of his way for as long as she decently could.

*   *   *

Polly came aboard to fetch a blanket to use for sitting on the grass and then joined Neil and Luke on the towpath to sit in the sunshine where bees murmured in the hedgerow.

Maria stayed below as long as she dared, long enough to hear Polly ask why Luke was painting here instead of working in the office back at the wharf.

'I was just helping out my brother yesterday.'

'Your brother owns the boat hiring place?'

'He does indeed.'

Stop it, Polly, Maria wanted to call out. She was sure that, for whatever reason, Luke objected to being questioned. Why couldn't Polly see it?

'Has he owned it long?' Polly persisted.

'Long enough,' said Luke.

To create a diversion, Maria carried the coffee tray up on deck and placed it on the seat, intending to go back for the biscuit tin before she carried it all ashore.

Luke leapt on board to help her. 'Let me.'

She let him take it, averting her face from

31

him as she went down below.

'The family business, you know,' she heard him say as she joined the others on the bank. 'I was brought up to it. My brother was keen to take over when our father died. All I wanted at the time was to go to art college. But, as I say, I'm around to help out at busy times.'

'Are you going to show us your painting?' Polly asked as Maria sank down beside her.

He raised one eyebrow. 'Painting?'

Polly slanted a mischievous look at him. 'Don't tell me you were sitting there pretending to paint. You looked engrossed in it to me.'

He shrugged. 'A few watercolour sketches, that's all.' He accepted a mug of coffee from Maria. 'I take them back to the studio and work from them there in oils or acrylics.'

'D'you sell your paintings?' asked Polly.

'It's part of my living. A secondary part, but important.'

'Then you must be good, mustn't he, Neil?'

All this time Neil had been staring dreamily at the white hawthorn blossom floating down every now and again like confetti from the branches overhanging the canal.

He started at Polly's voice and then smiled. 'I saw the poster for an Open Studio Event in the Bemerton area,' he said.

Luke smiled. 'The weekend after next if you're interested.'

'Maria's interested in art,' said Polly.

'Always at exhibitions in London, aren't you, Maria?'

Maria shot her sister a look of alarm, willing her to keep quiet. No prizes for guessing what her sister was up to, and apart from that, the conviction was growing on her that it wasn't a coincidence that Luke was sketching here.

But Polly wasn't to be deterred. 'She's always been interested in art, haven't you, Maria?'

Neil gave an exclamation of annoyance as he knocked his coffee mug flying. Glad of the excuse for action, Maria leapt up to refill it.

*　　*　　*

When she came back Luke was leaning on one elbow, chewing a piece of grass, and Polly was asking him if he lived in Yarnley.

'No I live in Bemerton. Right in the marina,' he told her. 'We hire boats from both wharfs so I've no problem getting to work in the mornings.'

'Fancy a lift on board *Dreamcatcher* to the next place you want to sketch?' Polly asked enthusiastically.

To her horror Maria felt herself flush. Polly was so obvious. Was that why Neil had caused the diversion? She shot a look at him and saw that he was gazing at a mother moorhen and two fluffy chicks that were pottering about near the opposite bank.

33

'I'm fine here for the moment, thanks,' said Luke easily. 'I'll get to the next lock on this stretch before you I expect, going by road. I want to paint the old stone bridge and the lock near it.'

He swung round as Maria approached and looked at her questioningly.

She felt the colour flood her face. Suppose he thought she had put her sister up to all this questioning?

'Maybe we should get on,' said Neil, coming suddenly to life. He got up and stretched.

Maria got up too and collected the mugs and the biscuit tin.

Luke helped them cast off.

'That was a bit sudden, wasn't it?' Polly grumbled as they got going.

Maria had had enough. She slammed the mugs down on the worktop in the galley and turned the hot tap on full blast.

'For goodness sake, Polly, leave things alone. You've got no sense. He's keeping an eye on us, can't you see?'

Polly laughed. 'Keeping an eye on us? Don't be daft. Why would he do that?'

'Isn't it obvious? His brother owns a boat hire company so he's bound to have all sorts of connections. I bet he's in cahoots with that other company who are keen to take over the boat hire business you're wanting to buy into!'

'For goodness' sake, Maria, I think you're being totally paranoid!' Her sister, joining her

34

in the galley and grabbing a teacloth, sounded incredulous. 'I think he's nice.'

'Nice? He wasn't very nice to me when I first met him. In fact he was downright hostile. And I think it's very odd that he happens to appear at this stage of our route, as if he was waiting for us to mess-up at the locks. Watching for us to make mistakes so he can report back?'

'But he's an artist,' said Polly, aggrieved. 'He paints scenes of bridges and locks and things.'

'We've only got his word for that. He wouldn't show us what he was painting, remember?'

Polly was unconvinced. 'If it's like you say, why didn't he jump at the chance to come aboard when I invited him?'

'We'd have wanted to see his work if he had. Blown his cover.'

'You're mad.'

'He'll be at the bridge by the lock as he said,' Maria said with conviction. 'Watching us.'

'He fancies you, that's why.'

Not even bothering to answer, Maria yanked the plug out of the sink and left the galley.

*   *   *

They moored again before they got to the next

lock because it was past lunch time and they were all hungry. While Polly was making sandwiches, Neil examined the map. He ate his food with a worried expression on his face.

'We may have gone wrong back there at that junction where the other arm of the canal joined,' he said.

'You mean we went left when we should have gone right?' said Polly, dismayed.

'Entirely my fault.' He stood up suddenly and knocked his head on the rim of the door once again.

'Oh, Neil,' said Polly in exasperation. 'Here, take this plate up to Maria and be useful. We'd better be quick eating and get off again.'

Neil ate his own sandwiches in silence, occasionally glancing at the map. 'I'm sure we've gone the wrong way,' he said when they had finished. 'But I can't think how we missed the signpost. Never mind, there's a winding hole up ahead if I'm right.'

'Winding?' said Polly. 'Wind to rhyme with sinned?'

'To turn round in,' said Neil patiently. 'But we'll have to go through the next lock to get to it.'

'We're losing valuable time,' Polly complained as they got ready to cast off.'

We'll make it up,' Maria said soothingly.

*   *   *

36

This time there was no lock keeper to help them with his advice. But neither was there anyone to watch them and Maria was thankful for that.

Once through the lock, Maria stayed at the helm as they headed for the section of canal that formed a pool wide enough for them to turn round. This was the winding pool. Then it was Polly and Neil's turn to do their bit with the lock gates once more. Then they were through and heading back the way they had come.

'Can't we go faster?' Polly complained.

'Don't be so impatient, Poll,' said Neil. 'Maria's keeping her cool. Why can't you?'

'Maria's not me, that's why,' said Polly, scowling.

Every now and again the canal narrowed as they went round a bend and they had to move out of the way of overhanging branches. They reached the junction again and this time took the correct arm.

'Thank goodness for that,' said Polly, her good temper restored.

They passed beneath bridges, all different and all with their number plaques on either side.

They had seen only a couple of other boats since leaving Leverton Locks. A heron flew alongside them for a while and then vanished over some tall trees.

'We've been going a long time,' said Neil

37

glancing at his watch. 'How about a stop for a meal . . . or even to tie-up for the night?'

'One more bridge,' said Maria.

'The next one has a lock soon after it,' said Polly, studying the map.

'Fine,' said Neil. 'We can cope with the lock in the morning. Agreed?'

'Agreed,' the girls chorused.

Polly looked up hopefully. 'This must be the bridge Luke said was his next painting place.'

Maria had already realised that. She would see him again, like it or not. She gripped the tiller determinedly. She was going to call his bluff and demand to see what he was working on. He wasn't going to get away with any excuses this time.

They slowed down as they neared the bridge and she looked ahead intently, expecting to see Luke's now familiar figure seated at his easel on the other side with his fair head bent in concentration.

An unexpected shimmer of disappointment ran through her when she saw that he wasn't there. But how could that be when she disliked him so much?

Pondering on that, she handed over the tiller to Neil, then picked up the mooring pegs and mallet ready to jump off as he brought *Dreamcatcher* carefully to the bank.

DISASTER STRIKES!

Maria was first up next day. She pulled aside the curtain in the galley and peered out. Rain streamed down the window and the world outside looked bleak. Even the passing ducks seemed depressed.

The bedroom door opened and Polly appeared, yawning. 'So . . . a dreary day weatherwise,' she said. 'I hope it won't hold us up too much.'

Maria grabbed the kettle and filled it with water. 'First things first.'

They sat on stools at the breakfast bar to drink their coffee, listening to the patter of rain on the roof.

'I suppose I'd better wake Neil now,' said Polly as she put down her empty mug. But she made no effort to move.

Maria felt lethargic too. There was something about the weather that made the thought of a quiet morning attractive. But there had to be some action in case Luke appeared early with his painting gear to watch their every move for any mistakes they might make as they negotiated the next lock.

'We'd better get under way,' she said.

Polly yawned. 'You're keen,' she said. 'Desperate to catch sight of hunky Luke?'

'Absolutely not,' Maria said with scorn.

Polly laughed. 'Says you!'

Breakfast was a leisurely meal because of the weather, and afterwards, as the girls started to clear away, Neil went up on deck. 'I'll check the bilge,' he said. 'And the oil.'

*   *   *

Neil needed to be on his own for a little while and set off for a stroll along the towpath while the washing-up was being done. It gave him a chance to clear his head and get things into perspective.

He could have done without the dripping trees, he thought, ducking to avoid an overhanging branch. The muddy towpath was slippery in places and the bushes made it extremely difficult to walk upright.

The project of delivering the boat to Bemerton by Friday week was a bigger commitment than he had at first thought. There were miles of canal in front of them with many hazards—like tunnels, swing bridges and goodness knows what else. Polly's enthusiasm couldn't disguise the fact that they were novices at this game, all three of them.

He wasn't even sure that he liked the idea of living on a boat for virtually a fortnight, let alone moving it through the canal system.

*   *   *

As soon as Neil was back on board they cast off straightaway. The rain had stopped which was something, but the seat in the well-deck felt damp even after Polly had attacked it with a towel.

Maria stood at the tiller, edging *Dreamcatcher* away from the bank, confident now that this was easy when you knew how. They passed slowly beneath the dripping bridge and out to a fairer world on the other side. Shafts of watery sunlight trickled through the trees.

Neil picked up the windlass as they approached the lock, ready to jump out on to the bank when they were close enough. They knew the drill by now, he and Polly, and there should have been no problem. Maria remained on board, ready to steer through the lock gates when they opened.

Polly stood waiting for Neil to deal with the paddle. 'Hurry up,' she called. 'We haven't got all day.'

To Maria's horror Neil reeled back as the windlass shot off the bar and hit him smartly on the arm. With a cry of anguish he let go of the windlass and fell to the ground.

Polly cried out too, leaping across the top of the lock gates to reach him. Maria steered *Dreamcatcher* into the bank again and jumped off with rope and mooring peg.

Neil's face was white.

Polly, distraught, sank down beside him and

41

looked round wildly. 'He's badly hurt. What are we going to do?'

Maria's mobile phone was in her pocket and she pulled it out.

'An ambulance please,' she said. 'An accident on lock gates on the canal. Where?' For a moment she had difficult remembering what county they were in let alone the nearest town and the bridge number. She breathed deeply and took herself in hand.

'They're sending an ambulance,' she told Polly and Neil when the call was finished.

Neil was in no position to argue about the girls taking charge. The immediate need was for them to make him comfortable where he was on the canal bank. Polly rushed to get the picnic rug and a pillow.

'I'm not an invalid,' he gasped as she made him lie down.

'A hot drink, that's what he needs,' she said. 'I'll put the kettle on.'

'No, no,' he said, obviously in pain, 'I want nothing.'

'The ambulance is coming,' Polly shouted. 'Can you hear the siren? Oh please, Neil, darling, be all right!'

'Thank goodness,' Maria said, hearing the sound getting nearer by the minute.

They soon saw the ambulance cross the bridge and then the men were coming along the towpath carrying a folding stretcher.

'At last!' cried Polly, jumping up.

The paramedics took charge immediately.

'I'll go to the hospital with him,' Polly said when they were ready to leave. 'You'll wait here, Maria?'

She held Neil's uninjured hand, surprised that there was warmth in it.

'Oh, Neil,' she whispered. 'What are we going to do now?'

'We'll soon have him there,' one of the paramedics said.

But Polly wasn't reassured. Neil looked paler than she had ever seen him and there was so much at stake here.

*   *   *

When the ambulance was at last out of sight the silence seemed threatening to Maria. To give herself something to do she tackled the washing-up and then made some sandwiches for lunch that she packed in a container to place in the fridge.

She fished out an apple and took it up on to the well-deck to munch while she studied the map to see what lay ahead. Once *Dreamcatcher* was through this lock there were no more hazards for some miles as far as she could see. Thank goodness for that.

Even if Neil hadn't broken anything, his accident would cause problems they could well do without. With his arm bandaged, negotiating the locks could be a real problem.

She heard the sound of an engine and voices. The approaching narrowboat didn't slow down but wasn't going fast anyway. She saw the name *Club Sonek* on its bows.

'You're moored too close to the lock gates, love,' the man called to her.

'Can I follow you through?' she asked. 'I'm not too sure how to handle the gates.'

'You single-handed?'

'For the moment.'

He grinned as he brought his boat into the bank in the small space in front of *Dreamcatcher*. 'Not a problem for a girl like you.' He shouted down into the galley of his own boat. 'What are you doing down there, Bella and Sonya? Time for action.'

Two girls came scrambling up on deck, one with her hair tied severely back with a piece of rope and the other with long dark hair that swung from side to side as she moved. Both looked annoyed.

He indicated the windlasses at his feet. 'Get a move on! We haven't got all day.'

Maria picked up her windlass too and jumped on to the bank. So far Polly and Neil had coped with the locks while she steered *Dreamcatcher* into position so this was a good opportunity to see how things were done.

With two people to cope with the gates on either side of the canal the lock didn't take long to fill. Maria watched carefully, aware that on her own she would have to cross backwards and forwards over on the gates themselves, unless the others would stay to give her a hand.

It soon became obvious that this wasn't their intention. Without a glance at her, both girls boarded *Club Sonek* after the gates opened to let them out the other side and their boat surged ahead, gaining speed so quickly the wash from the stern crashed against the canal bank. An alarmed duck squawked in protest.

Maria sighed. Now for it. First she had to open the paddles in the bottom gates to let the water out before she could steer *Dreamcatcher* in and shut the gates behind her. Then the water had to be let into the lock from above.

Concentrating hard she managed to do all that needed to be done slowly and with great care.

*　　　*　　　*

Some time later, with aching arms and a dry throat, she brought *Dreamcatcher* through the lock without anything terrible having happened.

Thankfully, she moored in a suitable place and sank down on the seat in the well-deck to recover.

The yellow water lilies near the opposite bank looked pretty in the intermittent sunshine. Earlier she had seen plenty of their

45

leaves decorating the surface of the canal but this was the first time she had seen the flowers. She wondered if the flowers, like the leaves, disappeared beneath the surface when the water was disturbed.

Why hadn't Polly phoned? But perhaps Neil was being attended to at this very moment and her sister was in no position to use her mobile. Patience was called for here.

The sun was warm now and the shadows of the trees sharp on the still green water. Birds sang and she saw a heron flap lazily above the trees. She dared not think what might happen if Neil's arm was broken; his right arm. Best to leave the worry of that until they were back again, he and Polly.

The faint sound of an engine alerted her to a narrowboat approaching. As it got closer the engine note changed as the boat slowed down to pass.

The elderly woman at the tiller gave a wave. 'Hello there,' she called.

'Hi,' said Maria, smiling.

The alarmed water lilies folded their leaves and, with the flowers, disappeared beneath the surface until danger was passed. Then they bobbed up again. Fascinated, Maria waited expectantly for more boats to come by so she could watch the plants doing this again.

*   *   *

'Trouble?' Luke asked blandly. Maria took a moment to still the beating of her heart. Seeing him so suddenly on the towpath was unexpected though she wasn't surprised to find he was somewhere in the vicinity. He stood there smiling at her, a rucksack on his back.

'Why should there be trouble?' she asked.

'Just asking.'

Wishful thinking on his part, of course. He would probably be only too pleased if they had to give up and go home.

'You've chosen an idyllic place to moor,' he commented.

'It's lovely here,' said Maria. It was no concern of his that her sister and brother-in-law had gone off to hospital after a nasty accident. She wasn't going to mention it.

'Are you wanting Polly or Neil?' She waved her hand vaguely in the direction of the bridge. 'They're off somewhere. I hope they won't be long.'

With luck she sounded suitably nonchalant. It was now nearly two hours since the ambulance crew had left, carrying Neil on the stretcher. She dared not think what the length of time might mean.

'I see.'

'It's allowed, isn't it . . . to go off and leave the boat? And I'm here to repel all boarders.'

He shot her a hurt look. 'You don't need to worry about me! I'm not about to leap on board and pillage the place.'

The expression on his face was so comical she couldn't help smiling.

'That's better,' he said, smiling too. 'Seriously though, you'd tell me if you couldn't cope with all this?'

'Absolutely.'

He looked so sympathetic standing there with his fair head on one side and a smile in his eyes that she was almost tempted to pour out all her fears. Talking things over with someone else would be such a relief. But not Luke. She dare not risk it. She was sure that for some reason he was keeping an eye on them, hoping for them to fail.

'So your sister and brother-in-law have gone for a stroll?'

She gulped, hoping the warmth in her face wouldn't seem like a guilty blush.

'Something like that.'

'I see.'

He didn't, of course, but he mustn't know that.

There was silence between them. What was he carrying about in that bulky rucksack of his? He bent to pick a blade of grass and chewed it as he looked thoughtfully across the canal at the belt of trees silhouetted against the clearing sky.

'I've things to do,' she murmured. She wished he would go. Neil coming back with his arm in plaster would be a dead give-away. In any case, her impulsive sister was likely to pour out all that had been happening immediately and not wait until they were on their own.

Luke looked up. The clear light in his blue eyes was disconcerting. 'I'm wandering along here looking for inspiration,' he said.

'More locks to paint?' she asked.

He shot her a suspicious look. 'Nothing wrong with that, I hope.'

Relieved, she watched him walk away from her along the towpath with his long, loping stride. The sun highlighted the top of his head as he passed out of the shadow of a hawthorn thick with blossom. She saw him pause to gaze at it. Then he moved on and was soon out of sight.

But with him gone the world seemed empty and a strange little ache in her heart refused to go away.

*　　　*　　　*

For some reason, Maria could settle to nothing. Would Luke come back this way soon and see that *Dreamcatcher* was still moored in the same spot and be curious? And, oh horrors, he might even decide that the narrowboat would make a good subject for his brush.

The tension was just beginning to get to her in a big way, when her mobile rang.

She whipped it out of her pocket. The rather gravely voice that spoke nearly made her drop the phone into the canal in shock.

Gary! She hadn't thought to hear Gary's voice ever again.

Her hand trembled.

'Hi there, Maria. How are you? All right? I thought I'd give you a buzz to see how you're coping.'

'Coping with what?'

'With life in general. Now that we've split up.'

'I'm fine, thanks.'

'You are?' he asked, surprised.

'Why shouldn't I be? And you?'

'Me, too. I hear you're on holiday on the inland waterways.'

Now who on earth had told him that?

'Yes, and it's great,' she said. 'So peaceful and calm.'

This wasn't quite true, of course, but never mind.

'I could join you if you want? I've a free couple of weeks as you know.'

'I'm with Polly and Neil and we've no room for anyone else.'

'If you say so. It's just that I feel so guilty . . .'

'Guilty?'

'For messing up your life,' he said.

'How do you mean . . . messing up my life?'

'Now we're no longer an item it must be hard for you. Maria . . . are you still there?'

Of course she was still here but she couldn't

50

speak for a moment. Did Gary really think that her life was empty without him?

'Maria, are you still there? Are you all right?'

'Of course I'm all right,' she managed to get out at last.

'Let's face it, Maria. We were together a long time . . .'

'Five months, that was all,' she said. 'I've no regrets, Gary, in fact, I've never felt better in my life.'

'You haven't?' He sounded surprised.

Suddenly she wanted him off the phone and out of her life.

'There's absolutely no need for you to be concerned about me,' she said. 'And now I must go.'

She ended the call and pushed her mobile into her pocket.

Honestly, the sheer arrogance of the man!

A few moments later her mobile rang again. This time the call was from Polly. Maria took a deep breath and struggled to keep calm.

'Where are you now,' she said. 'What's been happening?'

'It's not good news,' said Polly, her voice sounding distant and weak. 'They're keeping Neil in overnight. It's a bad break.'

'Are you still at the hospital? Shall I come . . .?' Maria broke off, knowing what a foolish suggestion it was when she had no transport.

'I'll be back with you as soon as I can,

Maria. I'll get a taxi to the wharf and pick up the car.'

'You'll have to park it a long way away from here,' Maria said anxiously. '*Dreamcatcher*'s at a different mooring now, further away from the road. It might not be safe to leave it so far away.'

She had sudden inspiration. 'Give me a minute or two to look at the map in case there's a better way to do it. OK?'

'But, Maria . . .'

'Don't worry. I'll get back to you.'

Moments later, with the map spread out in front of her on the table, she called her sister. 'It's like I thought,' she said. 'Bridge thirty-seven is the place for you to get to, not much more than a couple of miles ahead of where I am now. You've got a map in the glove compartment of the car, haven't you? You'll find it easily. It'll take me about an hour to get there I should think.'

'On your own?' Polly sounded horrified. 'You'll be careful?'

'I can do it, Polly, believe me. And take care yourself. See you!'

After her hours of inaction a challenge like this was welcome. The thought of it calmed her after Gary's upsetting phone call. She went up the steps to the well-deck and breathed deeply. Then she glanced ahead at the still water of the canal. It was an easy run with no locks so what could go wrong? She had put on

52

an act for Luke and carried that off. She could do this too. No problem.

It took moments to leap ashore to disengage the mooring ropes and knock the pegs out of the ground. Back on board again, she took care to increase the engine speed slowly as *Dreamcatcher* moved away from the bank. Then, seeing another boat approaching, she steered carefully to the right. Once past that she steered back into the centre again and increased her speed.

So far so good. This was easy enough. The banks slid past. She felt sure she would sooner or later come upon Luke painting on the canal bank. It wouldn't be a problem though. She would give him a cheerful wave as she passed by, hoping he would assume that Polly and Neil were down below. She smiled, relishing the chance to prove to herself that she was able to carry off something like this with confidence.

Luke couldn't criticise her handling of the narrowboat so far. No-one could. For an instant she thought of Gary and the time she had backed her car into a fence post at their favourite picnic spot down by the river. It had been a foggy day and she thought of the expression of Gary's face at the first crunch of the car. No big deal really, just a silly thing to happen.

But why remember that now? A trivial incident that had no bearing on their eventual break-up. The end of their relationship was a wound she thought she had got over but which stabbed her sometimes without warning.

On she went beneath two more bridges with no-one around to criticise her, not even Luke. So where was he? He had walked a long way . . . as far as this? Well, maybe.

The next bridge was bridge thirty-seven. This was it then. She had almost arrived at her destination.

STRUGGLING ON

Maria cut back the engine and steered beneath the bridge so slowly the boat hardly seemed to be moving. The trees were further from the canal here and the grassy towpath had been cut short for some distance.

She edged towards the bank. Once ashore she pulled on the central mooring rope expecting *Dreamcatcher* to come closer. Nothing happened. The narrowboat should have glided in the rest of the way with ease. Pull as she might, Maria was unable to budge *Dreamcatcher.* Now what was she to do?

She knew a moment's panic. Then she heard the engine of a car. She was still standing with the rope taut when Polly appeared on the towpath.

'Thank goodness you've come,' said Maria

54

breathlessly.

Polly took in the situation with a glance. 'In the nick of time, it seems,' she said. 'Here, give me the rope.'

'Why are they keeping Neil in overnight?' Maria asked immediately. 'He's OK?'

Polly nodded, grabbing the rope and tugging with all her strength. 'Checking on him, that's all. I'm not worried, really.' Her voice wobbled.

'Says you!' Maria scolded. Polly's face was chalk white.

'What are we meant to be doing?' said Polly, her voice stronger now. 'We can't stay here like this all night.'

Maria looked down into the water and saw the mud. 'It's too shallow here,' she said. 'How could I have been so stupid?'

'We're novices at this, that's why,' Polly said. Suddenly she looked even more deflated.

'Help me pull the boat further along,' Maria said, sorry that she had worried her sister when she was obviously concerned about Neil.

*　　　*　　　*

Between them they manoeuvred *Dreamcatcher* to where the water was deep enough for the boat to float close.

'Phew!' Maria said in relief when they had moored successfully. She followed Polly down the steps and flopped on to the nearest seat.

'So tell me exactly what they said at the hospital.'

Polly still looked pale and there were lines of worry on her forehead.

'Neil's arm's in plaster and he looks so ill. He's saying that no way can we continue after this. He wants us to give up and go home.'

'And leave *Dreamcatcher* here?'

'That's his idea.'

Maria was silent, thinking about it. How could they give up? There had to be a way out of this predicament somehow.

Polly's voice softened. 'Poor Neil. He's in a lot of pain.'

Maria looked at her with sympathy. 'Don't worry too much, Poll. He's still in shock by the sound of it. He may have a different view of things in the morning. Did they say when he could leave hospital?'

'Tomorrow, I hope.' Polly sat up straight and Maria laughed at the determined expression on her sister's face. 'They'd better let him out or I'll kidnap him.'

'That's more like it,' said Maria. 'Think positive.'

'We've got to get *Dreamcatcher* to Bemerton without fail,' said Polly. 'That's what I told him.' Suddenly she seemed to droop again. 'They said it was a bad break. He'll be all right, won't he, Maria? He looked so white.'

'So would you have been in the circumstances,' said Maria consolingly. 'Wait till you see him tomorrow . . . back to his old self, I'll bet.'

'Suppose he really doesn't want to continue?'

'Let's wait and see.' Maria hated to see her sister so down. She leaned forward and patted her hand. Polly was still in shock about Neil's accident herself even if she didn't realise it. 'I know how important this is to you, Polly, really I do. We'll talk about it some more when Neil's back.'

Polly didn't say anything for a moment. 'There's something I haven't told you, Maria,' she blurted out at last. 'Don't be mad at me. Luke was there when I went to get the car from the wharf car park. I was a bit upset . . . about Neil and everything. So . . . I told him what had happened.'

Maria gazed at her sister in dismay.

Polly went on, 'He took me into the café and bought me a strong coffee. I needed that, I can tell you. He was so kind and sympathetic.'

'Kind and sympathetic? You have to be joking.'

'He's a nice man, Maria. Why can't you see it? So somehow it all came out about this dream of ours and how you came to help us when I asked you because Gary had dumped you and ruined your holiday plans. I had the impression Luke was keen to help us.'

'I'll bet,' Maria said bitterly.

'Don't be like that,' Polly said.

'I know you think he's some sort of spy,' Polly burst out. 'But you're wrong. I know you are.'

Maria drummed her fingers on the table top. Luke must have gone straight back to town after she'd spoken to him. He hadn't gone further along the canal to paint at all. So what did it mean? That he was checking up on them of course. And now he knew she'd been putting on an act by pretending all was well. What sort of interpretation would he put on that? She felt a devastating sense of humiliation. But Polly needed her understanding now.

'It's OK, Poll,' she murmured. 'No harm done.' With difficulty she tried to smile.

'He likes you, Maria.'

'I don't believe he told you that.'

'Not in so many words,' Polly admitted. 'But it stands out a mile. The way his eyes lit up when I said your name and . . .'

She sounded so hopeful that Maria couldn't bear it. She turned an anguished face to her sister. 'Oh, Poll, please try to understand. You know what I've been through lately. I don't need a man. I need a bit of space.'

Polly's eyes filled with tears. 'I was only trying to help.'

Maria was immediately contrite. 'I know. Let's call a truce on it, OK?'

She was rewarded by a weak smile. 'I'm hungry,' Polly said.

Maria sprang up. 'Sandwiches in the fridge,

loads of them. Stay there. I'll get them.'

*　　　*　　　*

She piled some on a plate and handed them to her sister. Polly's bombshell had ruined her own appetite. She found a bottle of coke and sat down again.

Luke would soon report back to their rival company that they were unable to complete their contract in time now with the accident happening so soon after they started.

Polly finished the sandwiches on her plate and helped herself to more. 'These are good,' she murmured with her mouth full.

Maria smiled briefly. Somehow they couldn't give up yet. Perhaps she could ask Gary to come and help, but she dismissed that thought at once.

They were finished, she and him, even though he thought she couldn't manage without him.

'Feel better now?' she asked as Polly handed her the empty plate. 'What do you say to moving on a bit to see how we get on? The canal winds in a wide arc here so we won't be much further from Yarnley than we are now. And the further along the canal we go the better.'

And the less likelihood of running into Luke, she thought.

'I suppose we could.' Polly sounded

59

doubtful.

'Then when we've moored at a new place near another suitable bridge, we'll walk back along the towpath to move the car. And there's a pub nearby where we could get a meal. It's marked on the map.'

'Sounds OK.'

'It's good sense, Polly. It'll cheer Neil up no end to know we've done it without outside help. And we can, I know we can.'

Polly's eyes brightened. 'You're very persuasive.'

Maria got up. 'Then come on, my hearty. What are we waiting for? We'll up anchor and away!'

She was aware of the rising confidence in her voice and that must have been inspiring because Polly smiled and jumped up too. Between them they disengaged the mooring ropes and pulled out the metal pegs. Getting away from the bank was accomplished smoothly. They were on their way.

*   *   *

Two boats passed them. *Dreamcatcher* was moving slowly now because Polly had realised from the map that they were nearing a tunnel.

'Three quarters of a mile long,' she said in dismay. 'Do you think we'll be able to do it?'

Maria edged the gear lever forward a little and they gained speed. 'Easy,' she said. 'We'll follow the other boats and do what they do. They'll check the tunnel's clear. We'll keep just behind them. No problem.'

She flicked on the switch for the front light, trying hard not to grip the tiller too tightly as she concentrated on the job ahead.

'Do you want your waterproof?' Polly called up from below.

Maria was glad she had it on as they went further into the blackness of the tunnel because of the drips of water from the roof. The boats ahead of them were dim shapes but it was good to know they were there and that they weren't completely on their own.

'I can't believe we're doing this,' said Polly.

'I can't either,' said Maria. 'I keep pinching myself to check I'm not dreaming. We're getting good at it, the two of us. Neil will be impressed.'

'He'd better be,' said Polly. She pursed her lips, gazing fixedly at the shape of the boat ahead of them. 'These two boats appeared just at the right moment, didn't they?'

'And their crews looked so happy and confident it cheered me up,' said Maria. 'They made it look as if there's nothing to it.'

'They could be right,' said Polly.

Gradually the circle of light at the end of the tunnel grew larger. The first boat was out and then the second. When *Dreamcatcher* emerged, Polly came up from below, blinking at the sudden glare.

Maria pulled off her waterproof. 'Here, you take the tiller for a bit.'

She went down the steps and sank down on the seat nearest the door. They were doing fine. Even the thought of what lay ahead with only one person to work the lock gates didn't seem too daunting. Surely Neil would agree that they could carry on? Suppose Luke had offered to help them out and they had accepted? A warm glow seeped into her consciousness as for a moment she allowed herself to imagine how it would feel to have Luke on board.

But what was she thinking of? With an effort she tried to wrench her mind away from that possibility. It was she who had suggested to the others that Luke was watching them and was in the employ of the other boat company anxious to take over the firm Polly and Neil were interested in. But now a mischievous little imp seemed to be whispering in her ear: What proof had she that it was so? Suppose she had been wrong all along?

*   *   *

'We'll need to take on water soon,' Polly said. Maria grabbed the map to check the nearest water point.

'There's a marina further on,' she said. 'It's marked on the map.'

'How much further?'

'About a mile.'

'Quarter of an hour if we're going at maximum speed.'

'Dream on. It'll take us longer than that,' said Maria.

The banks drifted past. Trees gave way to open fields and then the landscape became wooded again. The other two boats had gone on ahead.

Polly, at the tiller, slowed down even more as they passed a moored boat.

It all looked idyllic.

* * *

Taking on water wasn't too difficult once they got *Dreamcatcher* in the right position. The marina consisted of a large pool to one side of the canal, with metal jetties at which several boats were tied up. Not a living soul was about. Polly hammered in a mooring peg to hold them in place while Maria unscrewed the cap in the hull near the front of their boat and inserted the hose ready for Polly to turn on the tap.

'It's like filling a car with petrol,' said Maria.

It was surprising how much water they had used and how big their tank appeared to be. Finished at last, they set off again, Maria at the tiller and Polly studying the map.

'There's a bridge round the bend with a pub nearby,' said Polly.

'A road bridge? That'll do us then.'

'So far so good,' said Maria with satisfaction once *Dreamcatcher* was tied to some handy mooring rings. She pulled shut the door and locked it.

It was strange striding out on firm land along the towpath back the way they'd come. At the tunnel entrance the path climbed up the hillside above it and followed a route across some fields to descend again to the canal bank. Maria was glad to see that Polly had lost her anxious look.

Once they reached the place where the car was parked, Polly unlocked the car doors and they got in. But before she had time to turn on the ignition a figure appeared alongside them.

'Luke!' she said warmly.

Maria gave a gasp of dismay as she registered who it was standing there.

'Hello again! We're just off back to the boat,' Polly told him. 'It's a lovely evening. We've walked miles along the towpath.'

He bent down to look through the car window.

'A message for Maria came through to the office.'

Polly looked worried. 'The hospital?' she asked sharply.

'Not the hospital. Don't worry. But we've been trying to get you on the boat's mobile and got no answer. Obviously, in the circumstances we were concerned.'

'What circumstances?' Maria asked boldly.

'We expected you to let us know Neil's state of health after the accident and to tell us what you intended to do,' said Luke.

Maria stared back at him. 'Why would you need to know?'

'We thought you might be staying near the hospital in Yarnley overnight and that would mean that *Dreamcatcher* had been left unoccupied. It's in the contract you signed that boats shouldn't be left unattended overnight, if you remember?'

Polly moved a little in her seat. 'Well, yes, but . . .'

Maria felt her cheeks grow warm once more. Luke had a point. She saw a dawning comprehension in Polly's eyes too, but her sister didn't take kindly to being in the wrong.

'Polly's sorry she forgot to phone the office to put you in the picture,' Maria said quickly before her sister had time to react. 'But she's had a lot to occupy her, as you can imagine. However, Neil does seem to be getting on well and should be ready to rejoin us soon. He'll be out tomorrow and then we'll be on our way.'

'That's good.'

He sounded pleased, but Maria wasn't fooled. Inside he would be crowing with delight, able to report back that things were not looking too good for them.

Polly smiled at him disarmingly. 'Can we give you a lift anywhere?'

He jerked his head in the direction of a Land Rover parked some way back along the lane.

'When we couldn't contact you I decided to look for *Dreamcatcher* myself,' he said. 'I was surprised to see your car here. I'm glad the boat's safe anyway.'

He didn't look particularly glad, thought Maria.

'Quite safe,' she said. 'And so are we. But thank you for your concern.'

'And there really are no problems?' he said. 'And you're on your way back to the boat now?'

An innocent question or one with deeper significance? Maria looked at him suspiciously and nodded. 'And you?'

'Back to base,' he said. 'We've a heavy day at the yard tomorrow. No sketching for me, I'm afraid.'

He seemed to be about to go off and then thought better of it.

'I nearly forgot that phone message. Someone anxious to contact you, Maria. Important, he said.'

'Thanks,' said Polly briskly, turning on the ignition. 'Now we'll be off.'

Looking back, Maria saw that Luke was still standing watching them. She retained the picture of his tall lean figure in jeans and white shirt long after he was out of sight. It was so annoying the way he lingered in her thoughts like this.

Polly jammed on the brake and the car screeched to a halt. 'But we didn't hear what the message was,' she cried.

'Too late now,' said Maria. 'Drive on, Polly. If it's important he'll contact us later.'

Obviously the message was from Gary, she thought, and she could do without hearing from him. With luck she would hear no more. She crossed her fingers tightly.

They set off again.

'I'd better check we're going the right way,' Maria said, pulling a road map out of the side pocket of the car. She glanced behind. 'He's trailing us! You'll have to pull in.'

Polly did so as soon as she could.

Luke pulled up behind them and got out.

'I forgot this.' He handed Maria a piece of paper through the window.

'Thanks,' she said crisply, crunching it in her hand.

'No problem.' He looked at her unsmilingly as if he could read deep into her thoughts. 'Take care.'

'You too,' she said, stuffing the paper into her pocket as they set off once more. They weren't followed this time.

DESPERATE MEASURES

Polly pulled off the road to park in a suitable spot near the bridge that was closest to *Dreamcatcher*'s mooring.

'So, what's this mystery message then?' she said as they got out of the car. 'Am I allowed to know?'

Maria pushed the paper deeper into her pocket, suspecting what the message was but not being prepared to get it out to check. She might have known that Gary wouldn't give up but his knowing so much about her whereabouts was disconcerting.

'It's just a note of a friend's phone number in case I need to call them. Which I don't, as it happens.'

'Is that all?' said Polly.

'Totally unimportant,' said Maria.

'If you say so. A lot of fuss about nothing then.'

Maria shrugged. 'That's right.'

For a moment they leaned on the parapet and gazed down at the narrowboat, so neat and compact alongside the bank.

Dreamcatcher had been their home for such a short while but already Maria felt fond of the boat. She also loved the smell of the trodden grass of the towpath and the quacking of the mother ducks calling to their broods of tiny ducklings. A week ago she hardly knew any of this existed but now the beauty of their surroundings tore at her heart.

'I'd hate to have to give up the trip now,' she said.

'Me too,' said Polly in heartfelt tones. 'I have to tell you I had a few doubts on the way to hospital. But I soon came to my senses. I'd really hate to give up now.'

'That's a relief,' said Maria.

'You don't regret joining us on this trip, do you, Maria?'

'Not one teeny, tiny bit.'

'Good,' said Polly.

They stood there for a moment more in silence, each deep in thought. Polly's face was pale, Maria noticed. Understandable in the circumstances but tomorrow she would have Neil back and things would look much brighter.

*　　*　　*

It was as well they were moored near a suitable place to eat because neither of them felt in the mood for preparing and cooking a meal for themselves.

The small dining-room in the canal-side pub was busy. They settled themselves at a table in the corner and set about studying the menu chalked on a blackboard on the wall.

'Something simple,' Polly sighed. 'Chicken

salad will do me.'

'Me too,' said Maria.

It was good to be able to relax a little after the day's events.

Maria tried not to think of Gary and the surprising phone call she'd received when she'd been waiting to hear from Polly. She'd have thought he would have forgotten all about her by now. She hoped he didn't think there was a chance they could get back together.

But away from the boat and with her mobile switched off, she felt safe from his attentions for the moment.

Their food came. Maria ate slowly, savouring every mouthful.

Polly finished first and then got up to go across the room to study the dessert trolley.

'Everything looks mouth-watering,' she said. 'I think I'll go for a banana split. How about you, Maria?'

Maria smiled and shook her head. 'Not for me, thanks, but you go ahead.'

She was glad to see that Polly's cheeks had more colour in them now.

She felt better herself now, too. The walk back along the towpath had done them both good.

Tomorrow they would be off early to drive into town so that Polly could pick Neil up from the hospital and then they could get on their way.

*   *   *

Maria was surprised by how quickly they got to Yarnley by car next morning. She was aware, of course, that the canal meandered about the countryside but, somehow, when they were aboard *Dreamcatcher* moving slowly along the canal, it was easy to forget this.

Sunlight sparkled on the road in front of them as Polly drove into the hospital car park.

'I hope Neil's ready and waiting for us,' Polly said happily as if she didn't doubt for a moment that he would be.

They checked in at the reception desk.

'Take a seat for the moment,' the receptionist said, smiling at them.

Maria had already found somewhere to sit and Polly plumped down beside her, stretching her bare legs out in front of her, and reached for a magazine from the pile nearby.

'Mrs Rankin? Could you come this way, please?'

Polly leapt up. 'Won't be long,' she called out to Maria as she followed the nurse along the corridor.

Maria picked up the magazine Polly had discarded. She had flicked through it and read a couple of articles by the time her sister and Neil appeared in the reception area at last.

*   *   *

71

Apart from his arm in a sling, Neil was looking more like his usual self. Maria was glad to see him smile. Polly, though, wasn't smiling. In fact she was looking so downcast that Maria was alarmed.

'Is something wrong?' she asked.

'You could say that,' said Polly as she held open the swing door for the other two. 'Just wait till you hear what it is.'

Maria followed them outside to the car park without saying anything.

'So,' said Polly as they settled themselves in the car. 'What's it to be? Coffee in a local café or back to *Dreamcatcher* for a council of war?'

'Let's get back to *Dreamcatcher* and talk there,' said Neil quietly.

'That's all right by me,' said Maria.

In silence, Polly drove out of town and Maria bit back the questions she was longing to ask. She could see that there was something seriously wrong by the set of Polly's shoulders. Neil said nothing. They should have been rejoicing that this unfortunate episode was behind them instead of looking as if the end of the world had come.

Polly parked the car and got out. Neil, in the passenger seat, didn't move for a moment.

Maria, getting out too, glanced at him anxiously. 'So what's going on?'

'Nothing's going on,' said Polly shortly. 'That's the whole point.' She opened the car door for her husband. 'You might as well come on board, Neil, while I pack.'

'Pack?' said Maria in horror.

'Doctor's orders,' said Polly shortly. 'It's home for Neil straight away. The end. Kaput.'

Neil looked at Maria and smiled sadly. 'I'm sorry, Maria. I've been told to go home and stay there. They wouldn't hear of me continuing on the boat.'

Shrugging, he indicated his plaster.

'You mean we've got to give up?' said Maria.

'Afraid so. Me anyway.'

'All of us,' said Polly in such a deadpan tone that Maria looked at her in alarm. Surely this couldn't be the end of her sister's dream?

Neil sighed. 'It's hard luck on you, Maria.'

'It's hard luck on you, too,' said Maria, trying to smile. She could see how upset about it he was.

'We need to talk,' said Polly grimly. She yanked open the boot of the car and pulled out two empty bags and a rucksack.

Maria took the bags from her so that Polly could support Neil as they went carefully down the steep path to the canal. Polly jumped on board first, unlocked the door and turned to help her husband aboard.

'Mind your head, Neil,' Maria warned.

Polly stumped heavily down to the cabin. Maria heard the banging of the wardrobe door and knew that her sister was taking out her frustration on the furniture.

Neil went carefully down the steps too, remembering to lower his head to avoid knocking it on the hatch cover, and sat down on the seat by the door. He was looking pale again and Maria looked at him in sympathy, wondering if he was in much pain.

'I'm too much of a liability,' he said.

'You'll never be that, Neil,' said Maria as she hurried to put the kettle on. 'It could have happened to anyone.'

'Polly wanted to do this so much and now I've ruined it for us all.'

She knew he was blaming himself for his carelessness with the windlass and there was nothing she could say to help him feel any better about that. She pulled out the table and when Polly came back they sat there to drink their coffee.

'So how are you really feeling, Neil?' Maria asked him. He'd made no comment about their location. Perhaps he hadn't noticed that the boat had been moved.

'Not so bad in myself.'

'So there's nothing else desperately wrong?'

'There could be if he doesn't take care,' Polly said darkly. She sat with both elbows on the table and looked gloomily down at her coffee. 'He has to keep still, you see, and it's so easy to knock himself about on board. As soon as the doctors heard about the narrowboat, they wouldn't hear of him continuing with the trip.'

'I can see why not,' said Maria.

There was silence for a moment and then Neil said, 'It meant so much to Polly, you know, doing this. To me too. Bad enough if I had to give up on an ordinary holiday afloat, but *this* . . .'

He didn't need to say more. Polly's tense expression was enough to convince anyone that the dreams she'd had were now gone.

Maria frowned. She knew how much it meant to them to have this opportunity to be part of the narrowboat hiring business at Bemerton.

'You've learnt enough already to know you like the narrowboat life,' she said. 'Wouldn't that be enough for you to be accepted into the business?'

Neil shook his head. 'Sadly not.'

'But if it hadn't been for your accident we'd have had no difficulty delivering *Dreamcatcher* to the marina by Friday week.'

'It was in the agreement that we should actually get *Dreamcatcher* there,' Neil said, his voice full of sadness.

Maria bit her lip, hardly knowing what to say. The trip had meant a lot to her too because of the opportunity it provided to help Polly.

She gazed out of the window at the gently swaying grass on the bank. Giving up would be awful.

But did it have to be that way? She had already proved she could handle the narrowboat. Maybe she could do something useful for them now.

'Can't I deliver *Dreamcatcher* for you?' she suggested.

Neil gave a short laugh. 'On your own, Maria?'

'Talk some sense,' said Polly. 'We wouldn't have a moment's peace knowing you were on your own.'

'It wouldn't be allowed anyway,' said Neil.

'There are a lot of helpful people about,' she said. 'I can get help and advice if I need it. I'm sure I can do it.'

'I can't see the people back there at the wharf being happy about that,' said Neil with a sigh.

'You're right, of course, Neil,' she said, sighing too. 'And it's a long way to go alone.'

It was no use saying that no one need know, because she knew that Luke would somehow find out. She drank her coffee and then collected the mugs to wash them while Polly stuffed the rest of hers and Neil's belongings into her rucksack.

'Listen,' said Neil, suddenly. 'I've got to be at home, but you haven't, Polly. Drive me home and then come back if you think you and Maria can manage to get *Dreamcatcher* to Bemerton. I can manage at home on my own.'

'Leave you at home on your own?' his wife

replied, and Maria heard the strain in her voice. 'I can't do that! You've just come out of hospital, for goodness' sake. You need someone to look after you.'

'I can manage by myself. And think how important this is to us,' he said.

Polly stopped packing and went to sit down beside him. She looked exhausted. 'But you're important, too, Neil. And what kind of hard-hearted brute would leave you at home to cope on your own?'

Neil sighed. 'I wish we'd never heard of this project.'

'Don't say that,' said Polly sharply. 'We did our best.'

'And now I've let you down.'

'Oh, Neil . . .' Suddenly Polly leaned her arms on the table and put her head in her hands. Her shoulders shook. 'I can't leave him on his own,' she said, her voice muffled. 'You do understand, don't you, Maria? And the doctor said . . .'

Neil put his uninjured arm round her. 'I know, love, I know.'

She raised her head. 'And now what's Maria going to do?'

Maria smiled at her with an effort. 'Don't worry about me,' she said calmly though she too was sick with regret. 'I'll go home, too.'

'We'll have to be off soon,' said Polly. 'And you'll need a lift back to Yarnley for your car. There's so much to do.'

'I can pack up after you've gone and leave it all tidy,' said Maria. 'Don't worry about anything except getting Neil home, Polly, please. Let me sort things out here for you at least.'

She got up, not wanting them to see how much she minded about it all.

Up in the well-deck, she sat down on the bench and gazed down into the smooth water. She'd been eager to help them because she owed Polly so much. And now that help was useless.

Unless . . .

She looked across the hedgerow to the low hills in the distance, peaceful against the sky. There was a plop in the water and some ripples spread in a widening circle . . .

Gary would come if she asked him. The thought was startling. She plunged her hand into the pocket of her shorts and pulled out the piece of crumpled paper with his message on it to read it for the first time. It was as she thought, he was begging her to consider getting back with him and wanting her to phone him to arrange a meeting.

Now, as she looked down at it, she remembered her dismay as Luke had handed it to her. Luke's handwriting was neat and easy to read. Unlike his inscrutable expression, she thought. What had he made of Gary's message as he wrote it down for her so carefully?

She reached for her mobile. Such an easy

thing to do, to phone Gary and ask him to come. Was it fair to rob Polly of her dream when a simple phone call could make matters right?

A NEW PLAN

Maria remained where she was for a few moments longer, thinking of the last time she'd seen Gary and of how troubled and awkward he'd looked when he'd ended their relationship.

'It's no good Maria,' he'd said. 'You must feel it too. It's not the same between us anymore, is it?'

Her split-second feeling of relief had been startling. She still wondered at it and at her calmness in agreeing with what he had been saying. Only after he had gone did she find she was trembling a little.

Now Gary's offer of practical help seemed proof that he was regretting their lost relationship. And at this time of crisis, Gary had been her first thought. Maria bit her lip, considering.

A fish jumped in the water and she watched the disturbance on the surface until the bubbles vanished and all was still again.

Asking for Gary's help was a big thing to do because she knew it would stir up old emotions

79

and this holiday with Polly and Neil, in such different surroundings and with people she loved, had begun to heal her hurt and her feelings of rejection.

Of course, she would have to make it painfully clear to Gary exactly what the position was on board *Dreamcatcher* and that theirs would be a working relationship only. Maybe he'd be quick to withdraw his offer of help when he heard the conditions.

She went back to the others.

'I've been thinking,' she said as she sat down. 'And I've come up with a brilliant idea. How about I get someone to help me out with getting *Dreamcatcher* to Bemerton Marina? Would that work, d'you think?'

Polly looked up, a hopeful expression on her face. 'You mean you'd ask Luke?'

Maria shook her head. 'Not Luke.'

'Then who?'

'Would bringing in someone new be allowed as part of the deal?'

Neil wrinkled his forehead. 'I don't think it would be a problem, Maria. Your name is on the contract as well as ours.'

Polly wriggled on her seat. 'Come on, Maria. Who is it? Do tell.'

'I've got someone in mind if you agree,' Maria said, rather hesitantly. 'I'll phone Gary.'

Polly jerked upright, astonished. 'You mean you'd ask *Gary* to come and help? But I thought you weren't in touch any more. So . . .

you've changed your mind about him?' She looked wonderingly at Maria. 'Are you sure about this?'

'He phoned me here when you were away at the hospital,' said Maria as casually as she could manage.

'He never did!' Polly exclaimed. 'And you didn't tell me.'

'I didn't know it would be so important at that time,' said Maria. 'He offered then to come and help before he knew what had happened. I turned him down because I don't want us to get back together in the same way. But this is different. It's not too late to ask him now.'

'And he'd drop everything to help us out?'

Maria nodded. 'I think so.'

Polly's eyes lit up. 'Oh, Maria! You'd really do this for us? It's great, isn't it Neil? It'll mean that we don't have to give up after all. And there's a chance I could get back to you for the odd day to help out a bit when you get nearer Bemerton. It's not so far from home to there.'

'That would be fine,' Maria said warmly. 'I'm sure that with Gary's help I can get *Dreamcatcher* to Bemerton Marina for you.'

'Think carefully before you ask him, though,' said Neil. 'It would help us out for sure. But what about you, Maria? How do you really feel about it?'

'I'll be fine,' she said confidently. 'Give me a

81

minute. I'll phone him now.'

*　　　*　　　*

She went up on deck to get a good signal and pulled out her mobile, heart thudding, to dial his number. She listened to the ringing tone, willing him to reply. But he wasn't answering. She would have to leave a message on his voice mail.

'I'll try again later if he doesn't get back to me,' she told the others, joining them down below.

'And you're sure he'll come?' said Neil.

'He's on leave from work, and he said he would,' said Maria. 'Of course he'll come.'

'And if he doesn't?'

'Then I'll have to go home, too,' said Maria. 'I can phone for a taxi to take me to Yarnley to collect my car. No need to worry about me. No need to hang around here either, you two. I'll be OK here until Gary arrives. I'll let you know immediately he gets here. Promise.'

Even then Polly was loath to go. But Maria, seeing the tiredness and worry on her brother-in-law's face, insisted.

'I'll keep in touch like I said,' she promised. 'Off you go, and good luck.' She hugged Polly and then, more carefully, Neil.

She smiled as she waved them off but as soon as they were out of sight her smile vanished. What had she let herself in for? She dare not think.

It was quiet without them. She switched on the television but the signal was poor. Never mind, she wasn't in the mood at the moment. She would try Gary again.

*   *   *

This time she got through at once. She heard the enthusiasm in his voice and she almost regretted her decision to ask for his help. Quickly, before she changed her mind, she explained the situation.

'It's a working relationship only, Gary. That's all it must be. We're friends now, aren't we?'

He seemed pleased, complacent even. 'If you need my help, Maria, of course I'll come.'

'I'd be eternally grateful.' She couldn't blame him for feeling a touch of smugness. He liked to be needed and in charge and he had already offered to come.

'But you hear what I'm saying, don't you, Gary? I'm not asking you because I want us to get romantically involved again. I'm just asking you for your help as a friend.'

'If that's the way it has to be then so be it.'

She smiled. 'So when will you get here?'

'Let me think,' he said. 'I've something on tonight but I could make it first thing tomorrow. Will that suit?'

'That would be great. So long as you're

83

sure.' Too much to hope he would drop everything and come straight away. He had agreed to come, that was the main thing. 'Thanks, Gary,' she said. 'You're a good friend and I appreciate it. That's what we are now, isn't it, good friends? That's the way it has to be.'

A short silence on the other end gave her a shiver of uneasiness.

'Gary?' she said. 'Is that all right?'

'If you say so.'

She had to be content with that, and also the knowledge that he wouldn't there until tomorrow. But so be it.

'So tell me how to find you,' he said. 'Where exactly are you?'

With the canal map open on the table before her, Maria told him which road to take out of Yarnley and how to get to the place where *Dreamcatcher* was moored. The journey would take him a couple of hours or more, but what did that matter when the alternative was to give up and go home herself?

By this time they should have been well on their way past the next staircase of locks and thinking of taking the right turn into the main part of the Grand Union Canal.

But never mind. Once Gary arrived, *Dreamcatcher* would be able to get on quickly and make up lost time.

*　　　*　　　*

With a feeling of relief she prepared a quick lunch, which she ate sitting out on the deck. Afterwards, once she had moved all her things into the end cabin and tidied up the galley, there was nothing else to do on board.

So . . . what to do to occupy herself? If necessary Polly could contact her wherever she was so there was no need to remain on *Dreamcatcher.* She would take a walk.

Before setting out she stood for a while leaning on the parapet of the bridge and looking down at the canal. It was a beautiful stretch of water and she loved it. Knowing she hadn't had to pack up and leave was a tremendous relief. She hoped Gary would appreciate its beauty and otherworldliness even if it wasn't the open sea she knew he craved.

The sound of an engine in the distance alerted her to another boat coming her way and she stood watching as it passed beneath the bridge. She waved to the helmsman and called a greeting. She watched until the boat was out of sight before setting off on her walk.

The narrow grass-edged lane looked intriguing and made a change from the towpath. Cows grazed in fields on either side. In the distance the low hills looked misty, and nearer at hand she caught a glimpse of water. She knew this to be a reservoir. It would make a good place to head for.

The water was so smooth that the reflections of the trees looked as if they had been cut out of cardboard and stuck on. A lovely scene to paint.

She thought momentarily of Luke, who'd be back at the wharf today helping his brother with the business.

It occurred to her, with a pang of dismay, that the office should be notified that Gary was taking over from Polly and Neil for the time being. This probably wouldn't have entered Polly's head, worried as she was about Neil and anxious to get him safely home.

So . . . should she phone the office herself? Not yet, she decided. Not until Gary came and they were ready to move off.

She thrust her hand into the pocket of her shorts to check she had her mobile with her and felt the screwed up paper containing Gary's message.

She smoothed out the paper to read it again and saw something she hadn't noticed before . . . a phone number with the STD code for this area although she didn't recognise this number as that of the office at the wharf.

Luke's then? It seemed likely but why? He had said nothing to her at the time. In any case he knew the number of the mobile belonging to *Dreamcatcher.* Nothing to stop him phoning her if he felt like it however much she didn't want him to.

Shrugging, she screwed the paper up again

and shoved it back in her pocket.

All of a sudden the beauty of the scene in front of Maria meant nothing. She wanted to be safely back on board *Dreamcatcher.*

* * *

But someone was there before her and was moving round the gunwale, holding on to the boat with one hand as if he was accustomed to walking round the outside of narrowboats and had no fear of slipping off.

She recognised Luke at once and paused for a moment before going down the steep bank to the towpath to watch and see what he would do next. He hadn't seen her, that was obvious.

With mounting annoyance she saw him return to the deck and examine the rudder, leaning over as far as he could so that a lock of hair flopped over his face. It was as he turned and pushed his hair out of his eyes that he saw her.

'Luke, what do you think you're doing?' she demanded as she ran down the path to the bank and stepped aboard.

His expression didn't change as he stood up and stretched. 'You're remembering to check the rudder every now and again, I hope?' he said. 'Weed twisted on it could do damage.'

'We don't need you to tell us that.'

'Checking, that's all.'

The cheek of the man!

'So you think we can't cope?'

'Your sister phoned to put me in the picture and I told her I'd come out to the boat at once.'

Maria frowned. So Polly had remembered about phoning the office. How she would love the idea of Luke rushing to her aid, Maria thought with indignation.

'My sister didn't specifically ask you to come and check up on me?' she said.

'She didn't have to. It's not far by road and I'd finished my duties at the wharf and was coming home this way anyway.'

'So it's company policy to check up on the boats all the time?'

'Don't look so affronted,' he said. '*Dreamcatcher* is my own boat after all. I've a right to feel concerned.'

Maria gazed at him, speechless. His own boat? So what was going on? Had Polly and Neil known this all along and kept quiet about it? Surely not. Her sister would have blurted out that intriguing piece of information straight away.

His face lit up in a smile. 'I've surprised you.'

But Maria wasn't smiling. She felt wrong-footed and she didn't like it.

'You have indeed.'

'All the boats are owned by someone,' he said.

'I suppose so. I hadn't thought,' she said.

'So what difference does my owning *Dreamcatcher* make? It's a narrowboat like any other.'

Maria paused, considering. Luke's owning the boat made all the difference in the world but she couldn't explain why. She looked at him through narrowed eyes. Maybe he was pulling a fast one.

'Why should I believe that you are the owner?'

'I'll show you.'

He leapt down the steps, pulling a key from the pocket of his shorts. 'Come down, Maria, and you'll see for yourself.'

She knew the wall cupboard was kept locked. She and Polly had made jokes about what was inside, imagining all sorts of intriguing objects. Now she saw that it contained books, most of them on British mammals. Luke flicked one open and she saw a name, *Luke Slane*, written in neat handwriting on the title pages. His name, of course, but where had she seen it before? There was also an official-looking log book. His name was in that too as owner of *Dreamcatcher.*

Convinced, she looked at him. 'So why didn't you tell us?'

'No point.'

'I don't understand. Why should your own boat have to be delivered to Bemerton by Polly and Neil?'

'The Open Studio Event is looming. I'm up to my eyes in preparation and I need *Dreamcatcher* in her home marina.'

'But why Polly and Neil?'

'My brother needed the mooring. I need *Dreamcatcher* at Bemerton. This chap needed the use of a narrowboat for whatever reason and my brother was glad to oblige.'

'Neil's cousin, you mean,' said Maria, thoughtfully.

'So why shouldn't Polly and Neil do the job?' he said. 'Someone had to do it.'

Maria wrinkled her nose, considering. 'But you don't altogether trust us with your precious boat? Is that why you always seem to be around, checking up on us?'

'Maybe.' His tone was inscrutable. He shut the cupboard door, locked it and pocketed the key.

'And is that why your brother and you were arguing?' she said.

'You heard that?'

'I could hardly help it.'

He shrugged. 'We were both tired and scratchy.'

'So what was the verdict?'

'What do you mean?'

'You were climbing round the boat to inspect *Dreamcatcher* on the outside. Did you find any gouges in the paint work, any gaping holes?'

He looked sheepish. 'Everything seems to

90

be OK.'

'And why shouldn't it be?'

'No reason,' he said. 'I'm sure you can cope. But what about this chap who's turning up to help you?'

'Didn't Polly explain?'

'Has he done any narrowboating before?'

She shook her head. 'Dinghy sailing is Gary's love.'

'*Dinghy sailing?*' he said, as if it was the lowest form of boatmanship. 'Are you sure he'll know what he's doing on a narrowboat? It couldn't be more different. Narrowboats are slow to respond, unlike tacking in sailing dinghies when you're switching from side to side with the wind roaring in the sails. You can smile, Maria, but it's not funny.' His blue eyes flashed.

'So you think Gary won't be able to adapt?' she said, her lips twitching in spite of her effort to control them.

Gary wouldn't think much of this criticism.

She remembered the time they had taken a pedalo out on Poole Park Lake and thought of bringing that experience up now for Luke's assessment. But a glance at his flushed face changed her mind. He seemed in a strange mood this morning.

There was the sound of a boat approaching but it didn't slow down to pass *Dreamcatcher*, and Luke's boat lurched with the force of the wake which hit against the bank.

'Ignoramuses,' Luke said in disgust. 'How can the wildlife be expected to cope with banks awash?'

Up on deck again, he glared after the offending boat. Maria saw that it was *Club Sonek* with the girl with the severe hairstyle at the helm. She noticed that they were travelling in the opposite direction to the previous occasions she'd seen the boat.

'They should be banned,' Luke said, 'roaring along like that and churning everything up.'

'Do you paint the canal wildlife?' said Maria.

He shook his head. 'You'd think I would, wouldn't you? But I love animals, especially those you find in this environment. You'll see otters if you're lucky.'

'Otters?' she said with interest. 'They live along the banks of the canal?'

'Oh yes, but they're shy creatures, keeping well out of sight. You see their spraint sometimes, marking their territory. Did you know that a male otter needs fifteen miles of canal or river bank?'

'I don't know much about them,' she said humbly.

He gazed across the water to the bank on the other side of the canal that had cow parsley and wild forget-me-nots growing among the grass.

'Maybe I'm too close emotionally to paint

92

them,' he said.

'But surely you need emotion in your paintings?'

Immediately Maria's doubts about him resurfaced. They only had his word for it that he was an artist and she had thought from the beginning that he was in the employ of that other company and looking after their interests.

'Emotion?' He shrugged. 'Maybe.' He seemed miles away from her in thought now and she stood silently, waiting for him to go.

*　　*　　*

As Luke walked away from Maria along the towpath, he wondered what had made him come out with that particular piece of information about his ownership of *Dreamcatcher.*

His brother, as authoritative as ever, had tried to extract a promise from him that he would keep it quiet for the time being. Although he had no intention of promising anything of the sort he hadn't meant to disclose it to anyone. Mark would be furious if he ever found out.

His brother, older than himself by nine years, had always been the assertive one and his father's favourite. It was Mark who was destined to take over the family business, the narrowboat hiring firm in Yarnley, when the time came.

Luke's own efforts to show any interest while growing up had been overshadowed by Mark's greater expertise.

To compensate, Luke had made the decision to go in another direction, to pretend that the canal system held little appeal for him apart from providing inspiration for his paintings. His time at art school had been a revelation. He knew the way his life should go from then on and for some time that had been fulfilling enough to see him through.

Then he had met Bella. His interest had been aroused not only in her but in narrowboating as well because her family ran a hiring firm and she liked nothing better than being on the waterways every spare moment she could take from her job as creative arts co-ordinator at the Arts Centre in Bemerton.

It was she who had involved him in the Open Studios Event, but by then their relationship had foundered.

An unexpected inheritance from a sympathetic aunt who had seen the way things were going as he was growing up had given him the means to purchase his beloved *Dreamcatcher.*

He plucked a piece of grass and began to chew it as he passed beneath the bridge over the canal and up the path to the road on the other side.

Thoughtfully he stared down at his

narrowboat moored against the bank a little distance away.

NEW CREW MEMBERS

It was well into the next afternoon before Maria heard a car slowing down and stopping near the bridge. Gary? She rushed up on to the deck. Of course it was Gary. Who else would stop their car there? Unless they wanted to exercise their dog, of course.

A black Labrador ran down the slope to the towpath and sniffed at a tuft of grass, his tail moving slowly from side to side. Not Gary then.

Disappointed, she turned away. How much longer would he be? And yet at the same time she felt unaccountably relieved that she was reprieved from coming face to face with him for a little while longer.

Since his last phone call, warning her that he was going to be later than he'd anticipated, she'd had plenty of time to think about how it would be, meeting him again. Would her old feelings come flooding back or was she well and truly over him now? She had thought she was. Now she wasn't too sure.

Mixed up, that's me, she thought wryly. She had been waiting for him for hours, feeling only impatience and a wish to get on their way.

Now she wished she hadn't asked him to come at all. She watched the dog run off along the path and expected his owner to appear, whistling.

To her surprise she saw someone in dark shorts and shirt come scrambling down the path. He had a huge rucksack on his back. Gary! Her heart seemed to rise in her throat and then subside. But why did he have a dog with him when he had always disliked animals, particularly dogs?

This one now ran back to him as he reached the towpath.

'Get down,' he said sharply, although the dog had made no effort to jump up.

Gary looked towards *Dreamcatcher*, seeming to take in everything about the boat at a glance.

'Hi there, Maria. Aren't you going to invite me aboard?'

'Oh, Gary, I'm so glad to see you,' she said with a rush. Her cheeks felt warm as she stepped out on to the bank to greet him, hoping he wouldn't misconstrue her invitation to join her on board *Dreamcatcher.*

'Boy, am I glad to get here!' He held her tightly to him for a moment and planted a kiss on her forehead.

She broke away. He looked just the same and it surprised her. But what had she expected . . . that he had grown a beard, changed his hairstyle? No, he still wore the dark colours he had always favoured, and his dark hair lay against his head in his usual style.

'Gary,' she said again.

'That's me. Great to be here when I didn't think I'd ever see you again, love.' His expression softened.

She flushed and looked away, indicating *Dreamcatcher* with a nod of her head.

'What do you think? Lovely, isn't she?'

'You're lovely, too, Maria. I think I made a big mistake in wanting to break up. I'm hoping you'll find it in your heart to forgive me?'

'Please, Gary. You know how it is. It's not like that any more.'

He looked so dejected she almost felt sorry for him.

'Friends only, as we agreed. OK?'

'OK,' he said, though he didn't look as if he really meant it.

'So, what do you think of *Dreamcatcher*?'

He walked alongside, his eyes narrowed. 'Not bad,' he said at last. 'Smaller than I thought.'

Maria smiled. '*Dreamcatcher* seems huge when you're trying to manoeuvre into locks,' she said.

'I believe you,' he said as if it was no concern of his.

He followed her as she climbed over on to the deck. Then he struggled out of the straps of his rucksack. 'Where can I dump this thing?'

The dog barked.

'Here, boy,' he said.

Maria looked at him in astonishment. 'Is he your dog?'

'Mine? Is it likely? You know how I feel about pets, especially dogs!'

'So why is he here with you?'

'I had to bring him. Too short notice to book him in somewhere. Not a problem is it?'

'But where did you get him?'

'He belongs to some friends I met since we split up. Or belonged, past tense, I should really say. They've gone abroad to work for six months at short notice and asked me to take the dog and try to find a home for him. Selfish, I call it, dumping the dog on me.'

'What's his name?' said Maria.

'Charlie.'

The dog's excitement grew at the mention of his name but he hesitated about jumping aboard.

'Stupid animal,' said Gary. He put down his rucksack and jumped to the bank to help the dog on to the boat.

Charlie sat down on the deck, grinning affably, tongue lolling.

Maria was grateful to Charlie for easing what could have been an awkward moment. She patted him, making a fuss of him. She still couldn't get her head round Gary looking after a dog. And a big one at that.

She stroked the sleek black coat and was rewarded by an enthusiastic licking of her hand.

'He's very friendly,' she said. 'Good dog. Sit!'

She smiled as Charlie obeyed.

'I'd better show you round *Dreamcatcher*, Gary, and explain a few things.'

She indicated the steps to the sitting area and followed him down.

With a scratching of claws on the hard surface of the steps, Charlie came too.

'So . . . you're on your own,' said Gary with a swift glance round. He made it sound a statement rather than a question and she didn't quite like his tone of voice because he sounded so self-satisfied. Well, she would have to put up with that. He was doing her a favour after all.

She turned her attention once more upon the dog who had lain down between the seats and was regarding her solemnly.

'He won't be any trouble,' said Gary. 'I'll donate him to you if you like.'

Maria smiled. She would have taken up Gary's offer if her small flat would accommodate both herself and a large dog. Charlie seemed quiet and friendly enough even if he did take up a lot of the available floor space. And Maria was glad to have him here. He was a third person on board *Dreamcatcher* and that was a good thing.

'I'll ring Polly in a minute and say you've arrived,' she said.

'So where do we sleep?'

Maria indicated the far cabin. 'That's my room at the far end. This seat turns into a single bed for you. I'll show you later.'

'Single?' His voice deepened with disappointment.

She glanced at him swiftly. 'Surely you didn't expect anything else, Gary, after what we agreed? You brought your sleeping bag?'

'Never go anywhere without it. So where shall I put my kit for the time being?'

'There's space the other side of the bathroom,' she said. 'Have you eaten?'

He nodded. 'I found a good place for a meal on the way up. I'll need to give the dog a drink though.'

'Have a look round the galley and familiarise yourself with the layout while I phone Polly. There are dishes under the sink.'

He got up to find water for the dog.

Charlie slurped noisily and then lay down again, his head on his paws.

Gary looked at Maria enquiringly when she'd finished her call. 'Shall we get going then?'

'There are things to show you first,' she said. 'A routine we have to go through each day, checking everything's in order and emptying the bilge. Water seeps in sometimes, you see.'

*   *   *

This didn't take long and Gary seemed happy with it all.

Suddenly Charlie leapt up, barking. Gary shouted at him to stop.

Maria, sticking her head out of the door to see what all the fuss was about, saw Luke on the towpath.

'Your sister didn't say your new crew member was a ferocious beast,' he said.

'Did you want something?' To her dismay Maria found herself stammering a little in her confusion. Luke wasn't carrying his painting gear. Had he come specially to check up on them?

She went up on the deck. Charlie followed her, still barking. Then his barks subsided.

'A good boat dog anyway,' said Luke as he stepped aboard. 'What's he called?'

Charlie gave a whine of excitement as Maria said his name.

'You do know animals aren't allowed on the boats that are let out for hire?' said Luke.

She looked at him in dismay. 'I hadn't realised.'

'Mmm.' Luke bent to give Charlie a pat. 'You're a friendly chap,' he said. 'Well-behaved, I hope.'

'And we haven't exactly hired this boat,' Maria said.

Luke straightened. 'Good point.'

'Polly rang the office again?' said Maria.

'All right and proper. But we need to have the details.'

He whipped out a notebook and biro from the pocket of his jeans and began to write.

She gave him the details of the new crew member, feeling awkward. He shot her an intent look as she told him Gary's name and home address and he paused in his writing for a second. All right and proper he had said so there was no need to justify her choice of companion. So why was she feeling guilty?

He snapped his notebook shut and looked appraisingly over the outside of the boat. Then he glanced at Charlie as if he'd like to give him a good hug.

Charlie's tail began to wag, hitting her on her bare legs. 'Hey, stop that,' she said, her voice light with relief that all seemed to be in order.

'I thought I'd drive down to see that all was well,' Luke said. He raised an eyebrow enquiringly at her. This gave his face a lopsided look that she hadn't seen before. She ought to be feeling annoyed that he was here checking up on her again but somehow she was finding it difficult. Maybe this was because Gary was here now and so there would be no worries about getting *Dreamcatcher* to Bemerton.

'Trouble?' Gary called up from below.

'No, not at all,' she said.

There were sounds of movement and Gary

came up the steps, bending his head to avoid hitting it on the hatch cover.

Maria hesitated. There was no avoiding it. She would have to introduce them.

Charlie slumped down for a rest after the exertion of welcoming Luke, taking up most of the room on the deck. He'd obviously decided that Luke was a friend. His tail thumped a couple of times as he grinned up at everyone.

Gary looked down at the dog with dislike, looking as if he itched to kick him.

'You two seem to be getting on well!' he said to Luke, indicating the dog. 'You're welcome to take him off my hands if you like.'

'This is Gary!' Maria said hurriedly. 'Gary, this is Luke, from the wharf office.'

Gary's nod was hardly discernible and Luke smiled a little distantly.

The two men could hardly be more different, Maria thought, looking from one to the other. Gary in his smart new shorts and sweatshirt looked like an advertisement for sportswear in a smart magazine while Luke's jeans were ragged at the knees and his shirt slightly crumpled.

'Know anything about being on the water?' Luke said. His tone was level but Maria knew what he was thinking.

'You could say so. The real water . . . the sea,' said Gary in such a patronising way that Maria wasn't surprised at Luke's frown. 'Sailing's the thing you know. Freedom to go where you will.'

'As long as there's some wind,' said Luke evenly. 'I hope you realise what you are taking on. Dinghies and narrowboats are poles apart.'

Gary laughed but he didn't sound amused. 'You could say that. I'll cope, never fear. And anyway, I've got Maria to keep me right.'

He put his arm round her and gave her a squeeze and she saw Luke's change of expression.

'We'll need to get on our way now,' she said quickly. Any more of this chattering and it would be doubtful if they started at all. 'We've lost a lot of time.'

Luke nodded. 'I'm on the end of the phone if you need me. You've got my number.'

She nodded.

'OK then, take care.' He seemed reluctant to leave but Gary's silence was far from friendly and there was a distinct chill in the air.

As he turned to go, Luke shot Maria another intent look. She thought she saw anxiety in it but that was absurd.

'Behave yourself, Charlie,' he called as he left. With a wave he was off up the path to the bridge. Maria watched him go with a strange feeling of loss.

'Friend of yours?' said Gary, watching Luke as he walked away.

'Hardly that,' she said. She wasn't about to tell him about her suspicions of Luke because she wasn't sure how he would react. His knowing that *Dreamcatcher* must be delivered to Bemerton Marina by next Friday was enough.

*   *   *

They set off very soon after Luke had gone, Maria at the helm as Gary released the mooring ropes and collected the pegs to leave handy on the deck for their next stop. Being under way felt good again. 'Like to take over now, Gary?' she said after a while.

She sat on the seat beside him as he stood at the tiller. The countryside slid past. Sunshine reflected from the water in flashes of gold, and the scent of honeysuckle wafted across to them every now and again.

'This is the life,' she said.

'It certainly is.'

'As good as sailing?'

Gary thought for a moment. 'Different. Nice. Especially with you beside me, Maria. It's almost like old times. Do you remember that time we took a punt down river? Picnicked under a willow tree if I remember rightly.'

Maria nodded. Why was he raking up that memory now? They had been at odds with one another that early spring day and it was the first hint that things weren't right between them.

He leaned forward to move the lever and

105

the wake streamed out behind them.

'Too fast,' she said. 'Slow down a bit.'

He took no notice and she hated the way the water washed against the banks in swirls of mud. A coot slid off her nest in alarm at what must have looked like a tidal wave coming too close for comfort.

'That's more like it,' he said in satisfaction. 'How long have we got to get to this place we're heading for?'

'Bemerton Marina,' she said. 'A week now. We've had a few hold-ups but there's no problem really. I'll show you the canal map when we stop for the night and you'll see.'

He nodded. 'You've got some food on board?'

'Enough for breakfast and some sandwiches. We could find a pub somewhere if you like. There aren't any near the canal for a bit but we could walk.'

'Sandwiches would be fine for me.' Gary slowed down as they passed some moored boats and didn't speed up again.

'This is better,' she said. 'Oh! Look over there!'

He glanced in the direction she pointed. There was a rustle of something near the bank, a plop as an animal entered the water and disappeared.

A line of bubbles showed its whereabouts for a while until they could see it no more.

'Is there much vermin around here?' Gary

said.

'Vermin?' said Maria in indignation. 'I don't know about vermin, but there's certainly wildlife, and plenty of it.'

She wondered if the animal they'd just missed seeing could have been an otter, but there must be plenty of other waterside animals that lived on the banks and she knew from Luke that otters were shy creatures.

*   *   *

After a while she went down to the galley and returned with sandwiches and mugs of tea.

'I thought we'd eat on the move,' she said.

Sitting together, watching the banks slip by felt peaceful, even though the chug of the engine drowned out the birdsong.

When they'd finished eating their sandwiches, Maria asked Gary what they should do about food for Charlie.

'There are several tins of dog food in my rucksack,' he said. 'Could you go down below and fetch one for him?'

She did as he'd suggested and then came back up on deck. 'I'll take over at the controls while you see to him. What about one of us taking him for a walk afterwards?'

Gary shrugged as she took over the tiller. 'I don't think that'll be necessary. I'll just turf him off the boat and he can run along the towpath after us.'

'What if he goes off somewhere on his own?'

'That's his look out.'

'But we're responsible for him!' Already she was thinking of Charlie as a member of the crew. With Gary in this uncaring mood the poor dog was was lucky to get a meal, she thought.

'I'll walk with him,' she said as soon as Charlie had gobbled up his dinner. 'Here, Charlie! Walkies!'

Maria strode along for some way, glad that she and Gary were no longer in close proximity. Charlie was enjoying himself, too, bounding backwards and forwards and exploring the longer grass by the hedge.

The entrance to a tunnel was getting near now. 'We'd better get back on board,' she called to Gary. 'It'll take both of us to get the boat through.'

'No problem, I'll take her through on my own,' he called back.

'No way!'

'Think I can't do it?'

'Gary, please!'

She couldn't bear *Dreamcatcher* to be out of her sight even for the fifteen minutes it would take for the boat to emerge on the other side.

'Stop, Gary. Bring the boat to the bank.'

'See you the other end,' he shouted.

The light came on at the front of *Dreamcatcher.* He meant it. How *dare* he!

She watched helplessly as *Dreamcatcher* headed for the entrance and then, calling Charlie, she scrambled up the path that led to the top of the hill, wishing that the towpath went through the tunnel too. The path narrowed between high clinging hedges that clutched at her hair.

All the time her anger grew until her face became hot and she was breathing in short gasps.

Suppose Gary met another boat and was going too fast to pass safely? It was such a stupid thing to do, taking *Dreamcatcher* through on his own.

Charlie was keeping pace with her as if this was some kind of game.

At last they arrived at the place where the footpath ran steeply downhill to join the towpath once more. Hardly daring to breathe, Maria looked into the tunnel and saw a light. By the time *Dreamcatcher* emerged into daylight she felt sick with relief.

Gary, looking triumphant, brought the narrowboat to the bank for her to jump aboard. Charlie needed no second bidding. He was getting good at this.

'Managed all right, didn't I?' said Gary, setting off again.

Maria glared at him. 'You could have got us into terrible trouble.' She breathed deeply, fighting for calm.

'Hey, you're not angry at me, blaming me

for something that didn't happen? Come on, love, we're not going to quarrel over it, are we?'

He flashed her the kind of smile that would once have had her anger melting away like snow in the sunshine. But not any more.

She glanced at her watch and saw that it was later than she had thought.

Dusk was beginning to fall.

'We'll have to moor somewhere soon,' she said. 'I'll take over now.'

*   *   *

To her relief, Gary went down to the sitting area and she was able to bring *Dreamcatcher* to the bank at a suitable place where the convenient mooring rings meant that pegs weren't required.

She made sure that all was fastened securely and then went below.

'I think I'll turn in now, Gary,' she said. 'Help yourself to a drink or something. I've put water in the kettle.'

'Will do,' he said. 'Goodnight, then.'

She heard him moving about soon after, assembling the bed in the sitting area.

Then she settled down, wondering what the next day would bring.

A NASTY ACCIDENT

Maria's dreams that night were filled with scenes of purple tunnels and flooded fields, all peopled with desperate narrowboat crews searching for their lost boats that seemed, miraculously, to be floating high in the sky above the marina at Bemerton, and *Dreamcatcher* was nowhere to be seen.

She awoke with a feeling of despair that was slow to clear.

She sat up, pushing her hair away from her eyes, and saw the sunshine pouring in through the window. Time to get up.

Surprisingly, there was no sound from the galley or the sitting area where Gary's bed had been made up. She used the bathroom and then dressed in shorts and a clean T-shirt before knocking tentatively at the intervening door. No sound. She knocked again.

It hadn't occurred to her that Gary might be up before her and his bedding cleared away. It all looked as neat as if no-one had slept there.

Neither was there any sign of Charlie's large body reclining on the galley floor so she guessed that both of them were off somewhere along the path.

She threw open the door and went up the steps to the deck, breathing in the pure air that she was glad to feel on her face this fresh morning.

The grass on the banks looked as if there'd been a shower in the night and there was the faint scent of honeysuckle that she loved so much.

A mother duck and her six ducklings swam by, disturbing the calm water.

Seeing Maria they swam hopefully nearer.

'Sorry, no food here at the moment,' she told them. 'Try again later.'

Losing interest they swam away.

*   *   *

Gary and Charlie had returned by the time she'd made coffee and had toast beneath the grill. She placed butter and marmalade on the breakfast bar and found plates and knives.

Gary's face was slightly flushed and there was a brightness about his eyes.

'Great day,' he said, wiping his feet on the mat as he stepped aboard.

Maria felt jaded in contrast with his enthusiasm.

Charlie flopped down, panting, at her feet.

'I'll get him a drink,' she said.

The dog lapped noisily and then slumped down again, getting in the way, but today Gary didn't complain as he stepped over him to reach the table.

They set off after Maria had washed-up and cleared everything away.

The air wasn't quite as warm as it had been the day before, and she shivered a little as she saw the black clouds looming on the horizon to the south, the direction in which they were heading. The wind was getting up too.

'It'll be raining soon,' Gary said. 'Those clouds are moving fast.'

Maria frowned, knowing that he was right. She went below to get her waterproofs ready and handed his anorak to him as he stood at the tiller. Then she thrust her arms into her cagoule and zipped it up to the neck.

Soon after that lightning flashed across the sky, followed almost immediately by a tremendous clap of thunder.

'That was close,' said Gary, ducking.

Then the rain came, dousing them in seconds.

'This is no good,' she shouted. 'We'll have to tie-up till it's finished.'

'Get down below, Maria, if you want. I can manage.'

'You can hardly see where we're going,' she shouted. 'Have some sense, Gary.'

'OK, you win.'

*　　　*　　　*

She grabbed the mooring pegs and hammer. By the time she had the ropes attached she was sodden, rain running down her face in torrents.

Down below deck once more, she quickly got out of her jacket and kicked off her wet trainers. Gary, too, looked as wet as if he'd been swimming fully clothed.

'Get the kettle on, why don't you?' he said. 'I'm going to take a shower.'

The thunder was further away now but the rain was as heavy as ever.

Maria, changed out of her wet things, made more coffee. Charlie, sprawled on the floor, looked up at her with interest.

'Good boy,' she said, giving him a pat. 'You had the sense to get yourself down here before the sky opened up.'

His tail thumped on the floor in reply.

The rain still pounded on the roof, sounding as if it would never stop.

Maria switched on the light because with the door closed against the elements it was so dark down there. Mooring beneath trees hadn't been a good idea either but they'd had no choice.

All she could think of now was their arrival at Bemerton, several days off. While making the toast for breakfast she had phoned Polly to report on their progress and to enquire about Neil. She hadn't mentioned the fuss about the tunnel, of course. Best to keep that to herself for the time being.

'I'll be able to join you for the day when you get near Bemerton,' Polly had promised. 'Everything's going great, Maria. I'm so glad

114

we've been able to go ahead with the trip.'

Maria had clicked off her phone, half-afraid of Polly's exuberance. There was plenty of time yet for something to go wrong.

*   *   *

They lunched where they were, to the sound of water dripping from the trees on to the roof, although, thankfully, the rain had now stopped.

Maria spread their sodden clothing over the shower rail to drip-dry, hoping the rain would hold off for the rest of the day so that they could make up the headway they'd lost that morning.

Gary, anxious to set off again, washed his plate and mug and then reached for hers.

'We'd better get on,' he said. 'We've wasted enough time already.'

The mooring pegs came up easily from the soft ground. Then they were away, with Maria at the tiller and Gary standing beside her. Being on the move again felt good after their enforced rest.

*   *   *

They chugged along for the next few miles. A few boats had passed them at their mooring, causing *Dreamcatcher* to rock a little, and they overtook two others on difficult bends.

115

'I like a bit of a challenge,' said Gary.

Maria smiled, glad that he looked more cheerful again now.

Narrowboating wasn't really his idea of fun but he was making a good job of hiding it.

'We'll be reaching a flight of six locks soon, won't we?' Gary said after a while. 'I'd better get the map to check.'

He brought it up on deck and spread it out on the roof. 'Yes, one more bridge and we're there.'

As Maria steered *Dreamcatcher* beneath an old stone bridge she saw what looked like a long line of boats ahead of them.

'Oh dear, this looks like it could be trouble,' she said.

Gary frowned. 'What's going on?'

Maria pulled into the bank. 'We'd better find out.'

She saw a group of people, waving and gesticulating.

'Something's obviously wrong,' said Gary. 'I'll go and investigate.'

He was away a long time.

Maria fetched their wet gear to drape over the tiller to dry in the open air, then she sat on deck to wait, cradling a mug of coffee. Charlie came up to join her.

She gazed across the canal, her thoughts thirty miles away with Polly and Neil at their home. Both would be feeling so frustrated and Neil, no doubt, full of guilt for the way that things had turned out.

In her mind she saw *Dreamcatcher* setting out from the wharf at Yarnley with Neil standing proudly at the tiller. A lovely moment and one she would cherish. But their hopes had been dashed so soon after. Thank goodness Gary was here to lend a hand and get them out of their difficulties.

A narrowboat came towards her, the noise of its engine startling her back to the present moment. The girl at the tiller shouted something, waving her hand to attract her attention.

Maria stood up the better to hear.

'There's a winding hole before the top lock,' the girl shouted again. 'They suggest we turn and go back because of the snarl-up, so that's what we're doing.'

'Thanks,' Maria called back.

*   *   *

Gary was returning now, looking serious.

'I don't believe this,' he said when he reached her. 'We're going to be stuck here for the night or even longer.'

She was alarmed. 'What's going on?'

He shrugged. 'Some sort of accident at the lower lock. They're having to get lifting gear in. It's a big job.'

'So it's serious. Is anyone hurt?'

'Not badly as far as I know but the

paramedics were there. Didn't you hear the siren?'

Maria hadn't heard anything apart from some distant shouting and low rumbles of thunder. She glanced anxiously at the sky, dreading a repeat performance of the storm that had hit them earlier.

'One boat has turned round,' she said.

'They're trying to get us all to do that,' said Gary. 'But I told them we'll just wait here and make the best of it.'

As he spoke another boat approached. The man at the tiller called across to them. 'You'd do well to turn around, mate.'

'No way.' Gary waved as the boat moved on.

Maria glanced at her watch. 'Another coffee?'

'Why not? While you're making it I'll get a third peg hammered in to make sure we're safe here for the night.'

*   *   *

Time passed slowly. Gary turned on the television but the signal was so bad he switched it off again in disgust.

Maria looked up from her magazine and glanced at her watch.

'Shall I make us something to eat? An omelette?'

'There's bound to be somewhere to eat round here,' Gary said. 'I'll go and investigate.

Coming?'

Maria shook her head. 'I need a shower. If you find somewhere, come back and tell me. Will you take Charlie with you?'

Gary looked at the dog with dislike. 'If I have to. Come on, boy!'

Charlie struggled to his feet and shambled after him.

Maria watched them walk along the towpath, Charlie stopping every now and again and Gary urging him on.

The thought of her own company for a while was sheer heaven after the strain of being in close contact with Gary these last few days.

*   *   *

In the shower she let the warm water cascade over her body in relief. By the time they returned she was dressed in her jeans and a warm jersey with her damp hair tied back from her face. She felt glowing and relaxed.

'Good news,' Gary said, looking a lot happier as he sprang aboard. 'There's a pub not far away and it looks a lively enough place. Everyone from the other boats that have been held up will be there, I guess. Let's join them.'

'What do we do with Charlie?' Maria asked.

'He's had a walk, he'll be OK left here. Hang on, I'll open another tin. He won't starve while we're away. Got any spare plastic bags handy?'

'What do you need those for?'

'The towpath's busy here. I'll tie them to the pegs so they show up and don't trip anybody walking past.'

She found some bags from under the sink and handed them to him.

'Good thinking,' she said.

He looked pleased at her praise.

Charlie lay sprawled on the floor between the seats. He appeared to be as happy to stay behind as she would have been. But she knew Gary would be offended if she suggested he went off to eat on his own while she cooked something simple for herself on board.

*   *   *

The pub dining-room was fairly full and noisy when they went in and Gary indicated a table by the window with a view over the canal.

'A gloomy scene to look at out there,' he commented. 'But we'll put up with it.'

As she seated herself, Maria noticed a painting on the wall, a bright canal scene in a myriad of brilliant colours. She gazed at it, feeling the atmosphere that the artist had caught.

Gary glanced up at the wall. 'Like it?' he said.

'Yes, oh, yes.'

He got up to look more closely. 'Pricey,' he

120

said in disgust as he sat down again. 'I don't know how they've got the nerve to ask it.'

She said nothing, wondering how a price could be put on something so incredible.

The waiter came to their table and during the business of ordering Maria wondered when they would see Luke again. She didn't doubt they would but she wasn't going to worry about that now. She was surprised he hadn't been round checking up again, though.

As they ate their excellent steak and chips she found she was enjoying being part of the crowd in the dining-room because the place felt cheerful and welcoming on such a dismal evening.

'The food's good,' she said.

Gary nodded. 'Surprising in a place like this.'

When at last they got up to leave, three people entered and headed for their table.

Mana saw that they were the crew of the narrowboat, *Club Sonek*.

'Over here, Derek,' said the dark-haired girl, smiling at Maria, obviously not recognising her, and then at Gary whom she did.

'Bella,' he said, delighted. 'And Sonya. What a shame, we've just finished our meal or we could all have eaten together. Another time, tomorrow night, perhaps?'

'I'll hold you to that,' Bella said, a dimple coming and going in her cheek as she gazed up

121

at him.

Sonya's hair was still wrenched back from her face. She smiled, too, and her face lightened in pleasure.

'Are you moored nearby?' Gary asked.

Derek grimaced, thrusting one hand deep in the pocket of his jacket. 'Nowhere else to go at the moment. A bad job at the lock.'

'Too right,' said Gary with feeling. 'It's too bad someone messed up. We're in a bit of a hurry to get to Bemerton.'

'What's the food like here?' Derek sat down and picked up the menu.

'Not bad,' said Gary. 'Don't you agree, Maria?'

Sonya and Derek turned to look at her and then away again. She had the distinct impression she wasn't actually here as far as they were concerned.

'Enjoy your meal,' said Gary as he and Maria left.

'Will do,' said Bella. 'See you.'

'I met them earlier,' Gary said as he stood aside at the open doorway for Maria to precede him. 'Nice crowd. They seemed interested in *Dreamcatcher* and where we're heading.'

'You didn't tell them why?'

'No big secret, is it?'

'I suppose not.'

'No harm done then.'

They walked along the towpath in silence. Maria, striving for something to say, was aware that they were both exhausted.

All through his coffee, Gary had been stifling yawns and she had to struggle against succumbing too.

'That was a lovely meal, Gary,' she said. 'Thank you.'

He looked pleased at her appreciation and her heart was touched.

He was doing her a big favour and she was grateful. 'I'd have liked you to have waited for me to go through the tunnel with you yesterday,' she said.

'I know, love, I know,' he said, smiling at her. 'Me too. I was a fool. Next time, eh?'

She smiled. 'Next time.' Though, of course, there wouldn't be a next time because there wasn't another tunnel on the way to Bemerton. But perhaps Gary didn't know that.

He took her arm. 'Like to take a look at the locks since we're so close?'

Maria nodded, freeing herself.

They walked down alongside the locks. At the bottom they paused. Deep gouges in the path showed where heavy equipment had been and one of the lock gates looked bashed.

She shuddered. 'What exactly happened?'

'The stern of a narrowboat going down caught on the ledge at the bottom of the gates as the water emptied. The chap with the windlass panicked. Instead of closing the paddles on the lower gates and letting more water in from the top he did nothing. You can imagine the scene.'

Maria could, only too well. The narrowboat with its stern stuck and its front dangling. They were all warned about this before setting off and Luke had stressed how important it was to keep *Dreamcatcher*'s stern away from the gates.

'Embarrassing for them,' Gary said.

'More than embarrassing,' she said with feeling. 'Someone must have been injured for the paramedics to have come.'

Gary shrugged. 'Shock only, I think. Their own stupid fault. Serve them right.' He gave a massive yawn. 'We'll sleep well tonight.'

Maria wasn't so sure of that after finding out what had occurred. This was the stuff nightmares were made of. She would take good care it never happened to them.

*   *   *

Gary paused as they reached *Dreamcatcher* and swung round to face her.

'Maria . . .' he began, his voice husky. He caught hold of her arms and pulled her to him.

Taken by surprise, she didn't move.

'Maria,' he murmured. 'I've waited a long time for this.' He bent and kissed her.

124

She pulled away. 'No, Gary!'

'Please, Maria, don't be like that.'

'It's not what I want. You know that.'

'I know nothing any more. Things change.'

She was close to tears. 'It's the way I feel. Please, Gary, try to understand.'

'Understand what?' he said bitterly. 'That I'm abhorrent to you? That you don't want me around any more? How about how I feel? Don't my feelings count?'

'I thought it was over between us,' she said faintly. 'I thought we were friends.'

'Nothing stays the same,' he said. 'These last few days have been good. I dared to hope that you felt the same way as me. Maybe I should pack up and leave if that's not the way it is.'

'You don't mean that?' she said, horrified. 'I need you, Gary, and you promised.'

He heaved a deep sigh and stepped away from her.

Charlie gave a low bark and came clambering up the steps to greet them and demand a walk as Maria unlocked the door. While Gary was obliging him, Maria used the bathroom and was already in her bedroom when they came back. She heard the sounds of the bed in the sitting area being assembled and then there was silence.

Stealthily she slipped out of bed and opened her door and whistled softly for Charlie. His presence on her bedroom floor snoring softly was a comfort.

CHARLIE RUNS OFF

Breakfast next day was a leisurely affair. 'I don't see any point in hurrying with all those boats queuing in front of us,' Gary grumbled.

'Another cup of tea, then?' asked Maria, standing up to see to it.

The throbbing sound of an engine disturbed the silence. *Dreamcatcher* rocked a little and the window darkened as the other boat passed them, travelling in the opposite direction to the one they wanted to go.

'One boat has got through the locks so things are moving,' Gary said with satisfaction.

'Hey, mate,' a voice shouted. 'Did you know two of your mooring pegs are out?'

Gary jumped up immediately and leapt up the steps to the deck. 'Thanks,' he shouted.

Maria, following close behind, saw with horror that only one rope was attaching *Dreamcatcher* to the bank. The front of the boat was floating out into midstream. Gary, muttering something under his breath, moved along the gunwale to catch at the central rope dangling in the water. He threw it to Maria who'd jumped on to the bank.

She caught the rope and pulled *Dreamcatcher* towards her. A few minutes more and they could have been in serious trouble. What might have happened didn't bear thinking about.

'We've lost the mooring pegs,' she said in dismay.

'Vandals did this,' Gary said, anger deepening his voice. He leapt to the bank, holding on to the rope attached to the bows. 'Here, Maria, hold this one too while I fish for the peg.'

It seemed an impossible task. She looked for the middle peg but the water was opaque and she could see nothing. She knelt down and plunged her bare arm in to feel for it. The water was deep here, too deep for her to able to feel anything down there.

'It's no good,' Gary said at last. He sat back on his heels, the sleeve of his shirt dripping water. 'I'd like to get my hands on the people responsible.'

Maria would too. She shuddered. 'It's horrible knowing someone crept up in the night and did this. What are we going to do, Gary?'

'We'll use the remaining peg to attach the middle rope for the moment. There must be something on board we can use to hook the other pegs out.'

'If they're down there,' said Maria.

Gary reached across and detached the boat hook from the roof.

'Stand back, Maria.'

He wielded the boat hook as if he meant business.

'I've found something,' he said triumphantly. 'It's down there with the plastic bag still attached. Just a minute, if I can just hook into the bag . . .'

A second later and one of the pegs was out, streaming water.

'Now the other,' he said.

This one was more difficult but at last he was successful.

'Well done, Gary,' Maria said as he knocked in the pegs.

He threw her a look of appreciation. 'I have my uses after all,' he said.

*   *   *

The flight of six locks that lowered the level of the canal by sixty feet presented no problem once they had waited their turn to proceed, but it was nearly noon by the time they got through.

They took turns to work the lock gates and steer *Dreamcatcher* into each level.

It was as Gary was steering out of the bottom lock and Maria was on the bank ready to board that she realised that an approaching narrowboat seemed in too much of a hurry to get past them into the empty lock.

'Watch it, Gary,' she warned above the noise of the engine.

'What?'

To her horror he wasn't moving over to give

enough room. The next moment there was a shuddering thud.

'Sorry,' called the girl at the tiller of the other boat, flashing a brilliant smile. 'No harm done, I hope.'

Maria hurriedly climbed back on board and leaned over the side.

'Oh,' she said in dismay when she saw the scratch marks on *Dreamcatcher*'s green paintwork.

The other boat, *Topsy Rose*, seemed unharmed.

Gary jumped ashore with the mooring rope and pulled the boat in close. *Topsy Rose* decided not to proceed into the lock after all and was mooring as well. There were two girls and two men on board. The girl who had been at the tiller jumped on to the towpath and came towards them.

'I messed that up, didn't I?' she said, still smiling.

Gary smiled back at her.

'On holiday are you?' said one of the men, jumping ashore too.

'Making a delivery to Bemerton Marina,' Maria told him. She ran her hand over the damaged paintwork.

'You are?' said the girl, her eyes bright with interest. 'Well, well. I'm Rosie and I know *Dreamcatcher*'s owner. Don't worry, we'll make it right with him when we show up at Bemerton.'

'A lick of paint will soon sort that out,' the man said. 'No problem. OK?'

'If you say so,' said Gary from the towpath.

He jumped aboard again with the rope and placed it on the roof ready for use next time.

'You're very affable today, Gary,' Maria said, still concerned about the scratch.

He grinned and waved to the crew of *Topsy Rose* who were now entering the lock. 'No real harm done,' he said.

'Good luck, *Dreamcatcher*,' the girl called.

'And to you,' Maria called back.

Dreamcatcher chugged along. The banks here were bright with clumps of red campion among the grass and Gary seemed happy. There was no looking at his watch today or urging Maria to go faster when it was her turn at the tiller. He sat on the seat beside her, glancing back every now and again, keeping watch for *Club Sonek*, Maria thought, with the girl Bella on board.

Well, so be it. This took the pressure off herself and she was glad of it.

After that they made good time and Maria went down into the galley to prepare sandwiches for them to eat on the move.

*   *   *

The afternoon wore on. Gary suggested he should walk with Charlie as far as the next lock. With his long strides he soon caught up

130

with the narrowboat that was just ahead of them and Maria could see that a good deal of banter was going on between himself and the helmsman as he walked alongside, ignoring the dog.

Charlie, left to his own devices, decided to investigate the long grass between the towpath and the canal. To Maria's dismay she saw him lose his foothold, slip and end up in the canal with a splash that sent water flying in all directions.

'Hey!' Gary called, alerted by the noise and turning back. 'Charlie, come out at once.'

But Charlie swam into the middle of the canal, obviously enjoying himself.

'Charlie!' called Maria.

The dog swam back to the bank and scrambled out just as Gary reached him. Giving himself an almighty shake, Charlie showered water everywhere.

'Stupid dog, now look what you've done,' Gary spluttered, leaping away from him.

But Charlie wagged his tail happily. It seemed to Maria, catching up with them in *Dreamcatcher*, that the dog was grinning. If she hadn't known better she would have said he'd done it on purpose.

Gary jumped on board as Maria came alongside the bank.

'I'll have to change,' he said, his face like thunder.

'Here, boy,' said Maria, encouraging the

dog to follow Gary on board.

Charlie, tongue lolling, sat down beside her, not seeming to realise he was in disgrace. Having him on board was great fun, she thought, and she patted him enthusiastically.

*　　　*　　　*

'Apparently there's a good place further on to moor for the night if we get there in time,' Gary said when he came back on deck. 'And there's a pub called *The Lock Keeper* where they do good food. What do you think?'

Maria yawned. 'Sounds good,' she said.

They moored behind another boat, relieved that there was still a vacant space in such a popular spot.

'Come on, Charlie, you can come too,' Maria said.

'He'd better behave himself,' said Gary darkly.

Charlie, realising at last that he was in disgrace, slunk along at Maria's side as they set off.

*　　　*　　　*

The pub tables that were set out on the grassy space bordering the canal were filling up quickly. The old building behind looked welcoming and attractive. Evening sunlight warmed the red brick and the small windows beneath the eaves twinkled.

'This is great,' Gary said, looking around in pleasure. 'Just what the doctor ordered.'

Maria was almost too tired to appreciate her surroundings by the time she and Gary seated themselves at a table large enough to accommodate themselves and *Club Sonek*'s crew as well.

'They'll turn up soon, never fear,' he said confidently.

Maria leaned back in her seat. For the moment they were alone and this was restful. Charlie lay sprawled on the grass between them, his chest rising and falling in heavy slumber. She thought that she would like to be doing the same.

'I'll get the drinks in,' Gary said at last.

While she waited, Maria put her hand to her mouth to disguise a yawn. It had been quite a day. Hopefully the others wouldn't be long because she could do with an early night. She glanced into the car park sited nearby behind some trees. It was filling up now, which wasn't surprising on a warm Sunday evening.

As she watched, a Land Rover drew in and the driver jumped out. Luke! She would know that head of blond hair anywhere. She saw him go to the back of his vehicle and lift out a bulky parcel. Hitching it up beneath one arm, he walked purposefully towards the door of *The Lock Keeper* and went inside.

She was surprised at the sweep of emotion

that ran through her like a rushing torrent. Seeing Luke was totally unexpected and yet why shouldn't he be here? She knew only too well that the canal wound about between places because of the lie of the land and that, by road, Bemerton was only a few miles distant. Her hands trembled and her throat was dry and she wondered that Luke had the power to affect her like this.

Gary returned with cider for them both. 'About time the others were here,' he said, glancing at his watch. 'It's getting busy in there. I think we should order.'

Maria took a sip of her cider then put down her glass. 'You need to order at the bar,' she said, getting up to do just that. 'What do you fancy, Gary?'

He had already made his mind what he wanted to eat so there was no problem there.

'The gammon please,' he said. 'And a couple of eggs on top. I'm famished.'

Maria went through the open door, blinking a little in the dimness inside.

She saw at once that Luke was over by the window, the parcel he'd been carrying was on the table between himself and another person. They both looked deeply involved in whatever it was they were discussing.

The brown paper on the parcel had been pulled away and several canvases exposed. Maria gazed across at them, loving the vivid shades he had used so extravagantly.

At that moment Luke picked one up and Maria saw the bright splash of colour more clearly. She had misjudged him . . . he was a painter as he had said. Some other paintings hung on the walls but the few gaps were clearly the reason for Luke being here now because they needed to be filled.

She bit her lip and turned away to place her order at the bar. Someone came up behind her and she knew it was Luke. Warmth flooded her face as she turned to look at him.

'I saw *Dreamcatcher*,' he said. Incredible how the huskiness in his voice was so disturbing. She forced herself to smile calmly at him. His business arrangements had obviously been completed swiftly. The pile of paintings that had been on the table were no longer there.

The lines deepened round his mouth as he smiled. 'Cope with everything today all right? I heard about the problem at the lock. A bad business.'

She nodded. 'We managed perfectly.' She was glad he hadn't been around to witness the collision at the bottom lock.

His smile vanished and he looked at her with an intent expression in his eyes that she found hard to bear. 'You'd tell me of any problems?'

As if, she thought. 'We're managing fine,' she said.

'Are you mooring here tonight? What have

you done with that dog of yours?'

'Charlie? He's outside.'

Luke nodded. 'And you're here with your new crew member?'

'Of course.' Maria felt awkward suddenly, wanting to ask Luke to join their party but hesitating in the face of his obvious disapproval of the new set-up on board *Dreamcatcher.*

He frowned. 'Don't let me keep you then. He'll be wondering where you are.'

She looked up at the painting on the wall behind the bar. The colours, mauves and deep blues, were blended in a way that pleased her. The scene was one of misty moorland, quite unlike the other ones of his of canal scenes she'd seen and yet she knew immediately that Luke had painted it.

'One of yours?' she said.

He nodded. 'I've more to do in the same series for the Open Studio Event in Bemerton that I told you about, so I'm pressed for time.'

'Of course,' she murmured. 'Me too. I must get back to Gary!'

He drew back, his face a closed book.

Outside again, she saw that *Club Sonek*'s crew had arrived and were already at the table being fussed over by Gary. They moved up to give Maria room and she squashed in beside Sonya while Derek went off to order for them.

Maria and Gary's food soon arrived.

'Don't wait for us,' said Bella. 'It'll get cold.'

Maria had ordered chicken but somehow she had lost her appetite. She glanced at Gary, seated between Bella and Sonya, obviously enjoying himself.

The dishes the others had ordered were soon to follow.

*   *   *

The noise and hilarity of the evening was almost too much for Maria in her exhausted state and she made up her mind to leave them to it as soon as she decently could.

At last Gary gave a huge yawn. 'I'm shattered.'

'Have a long lie-in tomorrow, why don't you?' Bella said, smiling at him. 'That's what I'll be doing, no worry.'

'Can't do that, I'm afraid. *Dreamcatcher*'s got to be delivered to Bemerton by Friday, early.'

Bella's dark hair bobbed round her face as she threw back her head. 'Two days should do it, easy. Less if you keep going.'

'That's not what Maria says.'

They all looked at her.

'Maria's too cautious,' Sonya commented, looking away again in a disinterested way.

'But . . .' Maria began, confused.

'Trust me, you've plenty of time,' said Derek, winking at Bella.

'Listen to my big brother, Gary,' said Sonya.

'Derek knows what he's talking about. We've done this trip loads of times. We'll be taking it easy ourselves if I've anything to do with it.'

'In that case I don't see any problem,' Gary said, standing up to get refills.

Maria felt a deep hurt that Gary should so easily believe them when he questioned all her decisions. She knew there was still a long way to go to reach Bemerton and tried to visualise the canal map as she sipped her cider. Had she got it wrong? She didn't think so.

She sat with her back to the row of trees that almost hid the car park but she was aware of the starting-up of Luke's Land Rover. She was aware too of it driving away. The silence she felt among the noise was deafening.

*   *   *

Gary was at the tiller two days later, looking happy and relaxed with Charlie sitting upright near him on the deck. They made a good-looking pair, the man and his faithful companion. Except that it wasn't like that at all. Poor unwanted Charlie! His tail hit the deck several times as if he felt her sympathy. Then he lay down and looked at her with soft brown eyes.

After clearing away the breakfast things, she pulled open the canal map and spread it out on the breakfast bar. They had made good progress yesterday after their late start but

138

they hadn't got as far as she had hoped.

The convivial evening at *The Lock Keeper* had a lot to answer for. Today there were five locks to negotiate. They must expect to be delayed as this wider part of the canal was busy.

She went to sit on the seat beside Gary. The sun was warm now and it was pleasant chugging along. A couple of swans swam towards them but soon went on their way again. Another boat approached and they slowed down while passing each other. Every now and again Gary looked behind. Was he checking up on *Club Sonek* and the girl, Bella, who was part of the crew? It seemed like it, she thought. She hoped they wouldn't hold them back.

They waited for another boat to come out of the open lock gates towards them and then Maria steered *Dreamcatcher* in at last. At the next lock they were in a queue of three, with boats needing to come down too. It was Gary's turn to deal with the gates and as Maria drew into the bank for him to get back on *Dreamcatcher*, he looked at Charlie with dislike.

'It's time that animal had some exercise,' he said in disgust. 'Come on with you, dog, get off the boat!'

Charlie, obviously annoyed at the interruption to his siesta, obeyed grudgingly.

At last they were out of the lock and on

their way again.

'Where's Charlie?' asked Maria suddenly.

'He'll find us,' said Gary as he sank down on the bench and grabbed the map. 'Three more locks to go and they'd better be easier than that one.'

'I can't see him anywhere,' said Maria putting the engine into neutral.

'What are you doing?'

'We can't leave Charlie behind.'

Gary looked annoyed. 'Can't we just?' He moved towards her to push the gear stick forward.

'No!' She struggled against him. 'Let me off. I'm going back to look for him.'

'You're mad,' he said, catching hold of her arms to restrain her.

She gave a deep, gasping breath. 'I want to moor and get off. Charlie could be in trouble.'

'Fat chance. Enjoying himself more like. The dog knows the score by now. He'll be back when it suits him.'

'Not if we're too far ahead.'

'I thought we were in a hurry to get to Bemerton?' he said.

He pushed the lever forward so *Dreamcatcher* gained speed.

'But we can't leave him,' she said in desperation. 'Bring the boat in to the bank. I'm getting off. You go on if you must, Gary.'

He looked furious. 'No way! If you go to look for that dog then I go home! Simple as that. It's your choice.'

She could see he meant it, but she didn't hesitate for a moment.

'I'm going to look for Charlie.'

He pulled the tiller round hard and they rammed the bank.

Maria was ready with the rope and mooring pegs as the bow swung round, giving her just enough chance to leap for dry ground. She heard Gary go down below.

By the time she had the mooring pegs in and had pulled *Dreamcatcher* against the bank to attach the ropes, Gary was up on the deck again with his rucksack packed.

'The dog's yours if you want him,' he said.

'Do you mean that?'

'Who cares anyway?'

'I care,' said Maria.

'But not for me,' said Gary. 'You've made that plain enough. I'm disappointed in you, Maria. I thought that when you wanted my help it would lead to us getting back together. I was wrong and it hurts.'

'I explained how it was to be,' she said despairingly. 'Good friends. You agreed, Gary.'

'Not in my heart.'

He thrust his arms into the straps of his rucksack and hoisted it on to his back.

'But how was I to know that. You can't let me down now. Please, Gary.'

'But you're letting me down, putting

141

Charlie's welfare before mine,' he said. 'You think more of that dog than you do of me. Admit it.'

She hesitated a moment too long.

'I'm worried about Charlie,' she said, conscious of tears welling. She swallowed hard. What was the use? She wouldn't beg any more. It was plain it would make no difference.

'Go then,' she said, her head held high. 'Make your own choice.'

'If that's the way you want it, I haven't any choice, have I? I'm off.' He stepped on to the bank.

She didn't need to ask where he was heading. Bella would welcome him aboard, she was sure.

LUKE AND GARY COME TO BLOWS

'Charlie!' Maria called and heard the rising panic in her own voice. She stopped and took several deep breaths, feeling very much alone. Gary was gone, Charlie too.

If only she could see that lumbering black body and fiercely wagging tail!

'Charlie . . . Charlie!' she called again.

She set off once more, walking swiftly along the towpath and gazing down into the canal, afraid of what she might see. He loved to swim. He might have become caught up in some hazard beneath the surface and been unable to extricate himself. But she saw no black body floating in the reeds and knew it was unlikely.

Oh, where was he? Suppose he had run off and she never saw him again? It didn't bear thinking about. She called again, less frantically this time, and was answered by a distant bark.

'Charlie,' she cried in delight. 'Where are you?'

She found him five minutes later close to the pathway that led up to a road bridge. He had collapsed on the towpath and lay with one leg stuck out at an awkward angle. He had obviously dragged himself down the path from the road with difficulty and was in pain.

'Charlie! Oh, Charlie!' she cried.

At once she was down on the ground beside him, running her hands over his panting body. He looked in a bad way.

'Oh, poor Charlie,' she said gently and was rewarded by a faint movement of his tail. She looked to left and right but saw no-one. He needed help, at once. They could have been a hundred miles from anywhere.

Charlie whined again. Quickly she got out her mobile, pulled out the crumpled paper Luke had given her and dialled the number.

She listened to the ringing tone, willing him to answer. When he did she couldn't speak for a moment for the lump in her throat.

'Maria?'

'Luke,' she said. 'Can you come? Please. At once. I need help.'

'Where are you?'

She checked the number on the bridge and told him.

'I'll be with you in five minutes.' He sounded calm and in charge. She hadn't told him what the problem was and he didn't waste time asking. He would come.

*　　　*　　　*

As she waited she stroked Charlie's sleek coat, feeling totally ujubilantseless. 'What were you thinking of, running off like that?' she murmured as she settled beside him on the hard ground. 'Suppose you'd been badly injured, killed even? We should never have let you out on to the towpath on your own. It's all our fault because we're responsible for you. At least, it's just me now.'

She stopped, instantly reminded of Gary. He had not only left her but Charlie as well.

That was her fault too. Gary had come to help her when she asked. She should have been more appreciative, more . . . She leaned her head on the dog's soft body and let the tears come. He gave a gentle whine as if he understood. 'Oh, Charlie, Charlie,' she murmured. 'Please be all right, please!'

Polly would be worried to death when she

knew what had been happening, Maria thought suddenly. Neil would be frantic too if he knew that Gary had left and she was on her own on *Dreamcatcher* for the rest of the journey to Bemerton. They would have to be put in the picture. With trembling hands, Maria pulled out her mobile again.

She listened to the ringing for some moments before Polly answered. Haltingly Maria explained what had happened.

'You mean Gary's walked off, just like that?' Polly's voice rose in indignation. 'But why?'

'We had a row about Charlie,' said Maria miserably. 'And now he's gone. I'm waiting for Luke. Charlie's hurt. Luke will be here soon.'

She could hear Neil's voice in the background as Polly put him in the picture. Then she came back to Maria again. 'Please don't worry, Maria,' she said earnestly. 'Give us a minute, ten minutes, half an hour. We'll work something out and I'll get back to you. Promise. Just see to that poor dog. *Dreamcatcher* can wait.'

Of course, Charlie needed all her attention now. She bent her head and rested it against his warm body, willing Luke to hurry.

*   *   *

After only a few moments she heard the sound of a vehicle pulling up and stopping. She raised her head as Luke came bounding down the path towards her. He took in the situation at a glance.

'What happened?'

'I think he must have run up to the road and collided with a car,' she said, her voice trembling.

'Let's have a look at him.'

Charlie's eyes had dulled. He whined a little as Luke knelt down and stroked him with gentle hands. 'It's all right, Charlie,' he said softly. 'We'll soon have you well again.'

He moved his hands over the dog's body.

'We'd better let the vet have a look at him,' he said at last.

'Is it far to take him?'

Luke patted Charlie and stood up. 'The Land Rover's parked as close as I could get it. We'll be at the surgery in no time.' He looked anxiously at Maria. 'You're all right?'

She nodded. 'I'm fine.'

'Good girl.'

Together they lifted Charlie and staggered with him up to the waiting vehicle and made him as comfortable as they could in the back. Maria was conscious of every jolt, even though she knew Luke was driving as steadily and carefully as he could.

She glanced at his tense face as they finally arrived in Bemerton and drew into the car park of the veterinary practice. She knew that he was as anxious about Charlie as she was.

The vet's waiting-room was fairly full but they didn't have to wait long.

'I'll need to keep him in,' the young vet told them after he'd examined the dog, murmuring words of reassurance to him as he did so. 'He'll need X-rays, but I think he's been lucky. Broken bones in his hind leg and shock, nothing more. It could have been worse, couldn't it, old chap?'

Charlie seemed to know he was in good hands but Maria hated leaving him. Luke put his hand on her arm as they reached the exit and guided her towards the Land Rover.

'Back to *Dreamcatcher*?' he asked.

'But Gary's gone,' she said faintly. Tears rose in her throat and she gulped, hating herself for her sudden weakness. She groped for a tissue to wipe her streaming face.

He paused. 'Like that is it?' He sounded concerned and not jubilant as she thought he might have been since she'd suspected he wanted them to fail in getting *Dreamcatcher* to Bemerton by Friday, the day after tomorrow. She raised her face and caught a glimpse of compassion in his blue eyes.

'It's . . . all right,' she gasped.

For answer he pulled her towards him and for a second held her close.

She took a deep breath, comforted by his strong arms and the warmth of his body.

'It's very much not all right,' he said, his voice terse as he released her.

'We quarrelled over Charlie,' she said, feeling better now.

'He left you with an injured dog, to cope on your own?'

'No, no. It wasn't like that. Gary didn't know. Charlie had gone missing, that's all. It was a huge worry for me. I was afraid of losing Charlie, that he'd get lost and wouldn't know where we were.'

'And Gary left you to find Charlie on your own?'

She nodded. It sounded bad. It *was* bad considering Charlie was Gary's responsibility. Tears filled her eyes again.

'Come on, let's get you back to *Dreamcatcher*,' he said. He opened the passenger door of the Land Rover. 'Jump in.'

Maria did as he said, still in shock about the events of the last hour. She struggled to put the mental picture of Charlie's injured body on the vet's inspection table out of her mind but couldn't. He had looked so vulnerable, so unhappy.

To her relief, Luke seemed to understand how she was feeling. He didn't speak until he had parked his vehicle near the bridge again and they had walked back along the towpath to the narrowboat.

'A hot drink first, don't you think?' he said as he stood back for her to step onboard ahead of him.

'You'll have one, too?'

'I think we could both use one.'

For the first time, she noticed that he was dressed differently today, in pale chinos with a light suede jacket over a dark blue shirt. To her dismay she saw a smear of Charlie's blood on one cuff and a grass stain higher up. But there was nothing she could do about it. She hadn't asked what he'd been doing when he received her message but, whatever it was, he had left it at a second's notice.

'Thank you for coming so quickly,' she said humbly.

'Charlie's going to be all right, you know,' he said.

He stepped on board behind her and she could feel his presence like a warm shield.

She half-turned towards him and tried to speak, to say more about how grateful she was that he had been there when Charlie needed help, but somehow the words wouldn't come. The next minute she felt herself folded in his arms.

'It was an obvious emergency,' he murmured. 'Of course I came. I told you I would help if you needed it.' He bent and kissed her.

For a blissful moment she let herself relax against him, breathing in the warm feel of his body against hers.

When he released her she went hurriedly

down the steps into the galley and pressed both hands down hard on the draining board to gain some calm. She hadn't really believed Luke meant what he said when he told her he would come at once if she needed help. But he had. She had believed only that he wanted them to fail and would be pleased if anything happened to make that come true.

She made coffee as if in a dream and they drank it on the deck, she on the wooden seat and Luke balanced on the rail with his long legs stretched out before him. He didn't mention Gary again and she was grateful.

She gazed down at her mug of coffee in silence. She felt lethargic, still dazed at the recent events. In this strange state it no longer seemed important to get *Dreamcatcher* to their destination or even that Polly and Neil might be concerned about her.

'Maria?' Luke said at last.

She raised her eyes to look at him. He looked so strong and capable as he gazed back at her that her heart was stirred.

'Have you food on board for an evening meal?'

She shook her head. 'Only some eggs.'

'Then we'll get some fish and chips and eat them at my place,' he said. The offer sounded inviting but she hesitated. 'But you're so busy with The Open Studios Event and the exhibitions . . .'

'Not to worry,' he said. He took a sip of

150

coffee and put the mug down on the deck. 'You look as if you need a good meal,' he said, smiling at her.

She glanced at her watch. 'Polly's going to be ringing me back in a minute.'

She jumped as her mobile rang.

'That'll be her now,' she said, picking up her phone from the shelf. She looked at the screen in disbelief.

'What's wrong?'

'It's Gary.' She held the mobile in her hand, staring down at it and ignoring the ringing tone.

'Aren't you going to answer it?'

She pressed the switch and held the mobile to her ear. 'Gary . . . where are you?' The noise in the background made it difficult to hear his voice.

'I was too hasty, Maria. I can see that now.' He sounded contrite. 'Of course we should have waited for the dog. You were right there. I admit it. The wretched animal could have caused a nuisance for other boat users and we'd have been liable. Maria, say something. Can I hear . . .'

The sound of blaring music cut out his words.

'Gary,' she said. 'I can't hear you.'

The noise stopped suddenly. She imagined him escaping through an outside door, the phone at his mouth.

'Is that better?' he said.

151

'What's he saying to you?' said Luke.

'Is that a man's voice I hear?' said Gary, annoyed. 'Who have you got there with you, Maria? Do I know him?'

'Where are you, Gary?' she said again.

'Sorry about the racket just now. I'm in a café in Bemerton. Maria, love, I can get back to you tomorrow morning, no problem. That's why I rang to put your mind at rest. You can rely on me, Maria.'

'I don't think so,' she said coldly. 'And I've decided to make other arrangements. So, no, thank you, Gary.' She clicked off the mobile and it immediately rang again. It was Polly this time.

'How's Charlie?' she asked. 'Did you get him to the vet? Is he going to be all right?'

'Hey, wait a minute,' Maria said, laughing. 'So many questions.'

'Well, that's a relief,' said Polly. 'I can tell by your voice he's OK. Thank goodness for that. I knew Luke would get things sorted.'

'The vet's doing that,' said Maria.

'OK, have it your own way. With a bit of luck I'll soon be seeing Charlie for myself, anyway. Our neighbours have offered me a lift tomorrow, what d'you think of that? They're planning a day trip to Yarnley to see their daughter and they'll drop me off where you are now and pick me up wherever we reach in the evening if I phone them with the details.'

'That's wonderful, Polly,' said Maria, her

voice light with relief. '*Dreamcatcher*'s near bridge fifty-one.'

'That's what I thought,' said Polly, her voice muffled for a moment. 'Hang on. I'll write that down to be sure.'

'You'll come early?'

'You bet. They promise we'll leave here at eight. Be ready to cast off.'

'I will,' Maria promised.

'See you then. Neil sends his love.'

*　　*　　*

Maria replaced the mobile on the shelf though she wasn't anticipating any more calls.

'That's wonderful,' she said. 'The problem of moving *Dreamcatcher* tomorrow is solved,' she said. 'Polly's coming down for the day. We'll do it together. Isn't that great?'

Luke frowned. Surely he wasn't unhappy about that because he'd had plans to scupper hers and now there wouldn't be the opportunity? But that was ridiculous. She was mad to imagine he had a hidden agenda.

He sprang up. 'Come on then, let's find those fish and chips before we collapse with hunger.'

'I've something to show you first,' she said, suddenly remembering the scratch in the paintwork that she had forgotten until now.

'You have?'

'You won't like it. You won't want to be

going for fish and chips with me when you see it.'

'Better show me then.'

She took a deep breath. 'It happened when we were coming out of the bottom of the six locks. We got too close to another boat. We collided,' she said quickly, afraid to look at him. 'There are marks in the paintwork, the side away from the towpath.'

He leaned over so far she thought he would fall. She stood behind him miserably aware that *Dreamcatcher* was his own precious narrowboat that he had obviously looked after so lovingly.

'Were you at the tiller?' he asked, as he stood upright again.

She shook her head.

His lips tightened. 'I thought not.'

'I'm sorry, Luke. I wouldn't have had it happen for the world.'

'I believe you. But don't worry, Maria. I'll see to it at Bemerton. Come on, let's get going. I'm starving.'

*   *   *

Maria knew that Bemerton Marina was only a small one but she was surprised at the number of boats tied up to the metal jetties that stuck out at right angles to the main quayside. Further along there was a place for other boats to moor. The buildings bordering the wharf had been renovated to a high standard. Offices, a restaurant, a chandler's and a gift shop.

They purchased their fish and chips in the High Street and carried the steaming bundles to Luke's apartment above his studio which was reached via stone steps that ran up the outside of a building situated on the quayside.

He unlocked the door and stood to one side. 'Welcome, Maria. A modest place but my own,' he said. 'At least until the end of next week.'

Maria looked in surprise at the numerous boxes scattered over the floor and at the curtainless windows. 'You're moving?'

'I am.'

'Are you planning to move locally?'

'Hmm,' he said.

She had the feeling he didn't wish to say more and so walked across to the window that overlooked the marina.

'Fabulous view,' she said.

'I shall miss it,' he said.

He was already unwrapping his fish and chips and the aroma filled the bare room making her mouth water.

'I'm going to use a box for a dining-table,' he said, pulling two chairs forward. 'Happy to do the same?'

He produced plates and knives and forks and they began to eat. She thought suddenly of *The Crown Inn* and the similar meal she had

155

shared there with Gary. The atmosphere here was far nicer; relaxed and friendly. They talked about Charlie and his accident.

'Charlie's going to be mine to keep, if I want him,' Maria said.

'Then he'll have a good home in Richmond. Are you near the park? That'll be fine for exercising him. He'll love it. A dog like that needs plenty of room.'

'I'm near the Thames, not the park. I love being near the water. I could move, I suppose, to a bigger apartment in a cheaper area.'

'What about your work?'

'I've been thinking about that for a while now. I've enjoyed my work as secretary in a large medical practice. It's interesting but I've been thinking I might like a change.'

'Connected with water since you love it so much?'

He was teasing her. She saw it in his upturned mouth and sparkling eyes. She smiled too.

Afterwards they washed-up in the kitchen and Luke made tea that they drank standing at the window of the main room, looking down at the busy scene below.

'We'd better get you back,' he said at last.

*   *   *

Fewer people crowded the marina now as Maria followed Luke down the stone steps.

156

The wind had dropped, too, and the early evening was pleasantly warm. It seemed a magic time between daylight and dusk.

The door of *The Noisy Duck* café on the quayside opened and a figure emerged. They were too far away to distinguish his features but Maria recognised the way he walked at once, surprised to see him on his own. It was Gary.

Beside her she felt Luke tense.

Gary, seeing her, came towards her. 'Maria, what are you doing here? If I'd known you were coming into Bemerton we could have arranged to meet. We need to talk.'

'Not any more,' said Luke, shooting out his right fist.

Gary staggered back, his hand to his jaw. 'What the . . .?' Then, with the light of battle in his eyes, he sprang towards Luke who was ready for him.

To Maria's horror a full-scale fight seemed about to take place.

'Stop it,' she cried, trying to get between them.

Aware of this, Luke pulled away and stood breathing deeply. Before Gary could gather himself for more, a couple came wandering round the corner.

'Trouble?' asked the man.

'Not really,' Maria said quickly, nearly in tears. She pushed at Gary who had the sense to move back.

'I'll be around tomorrow if you need me, Maria,' he said thickly.

'I hope that's an empty threat,' Luke said, his voice deadly quiet as they moved away.

* * *

Back in the Land Rover she saw her hands were trembling. She hid them in her lap so Luke wouldn't see.

'Don't let that little scene worry you,' Luke said. 'He had that coming to him. He'll leave you alone now.' He turned his head to look at her. 'If that's what you want?'

She nodded, unable to speak. The emotion of it all was beginning to get to her.

Luke drove silently to the bridge she was coming to know so well. Two other boats were moored there now, looking cosy with lights shining from their windows.

She was pleased that *Dreamcatcher* wouldn't be alone and this seemed a safer place than their mooring at the top of the six locks where someone had tried to set *Dreamcatcher* adrift. She had forgotten about that until now and was glad she hadn't told Luke about it. With his Open Studio Exhibition coming up he had enough to worry about without being concerned for the safety of his precious narrowboat.

'Don't get out,' she said. 'I'll be all right.'

He nodded. 'I'll wait until I see your lights

go on,' he said.

She looked at him anxiously. 'You're all right, Luke. Not injured at all?'

He smiled. 'All in one piece.'

'I'm glad,' she said simply.

POLLY PANICS

Maria leaned on the parapet of the old stone bridge, listening for the sound of the car that would bring Polly to join her on *Dreamcatcher* this fine morning. Polly had phoned earlier to say that they had set off at the time planned and that all was well. All Maria needed now was patience but that was hard to find when she was looking forward so much to seeing her sister and being able to get *Dreamcatcher* on the move again.

The other two narrowboats had moved off while she was eating her breakfast, the crews calling cheerfully to each other. She watched them go, envying them their early starts. Soon, hopefully, *Dreamcatcher* would be moving towards Bemerton, too.

'Come on, Polly,' she murmured. 'Hurry up! Time you were here.'

Down below her the water of the canal was disturbed by a family of ducklings, guarded by an anxious quacking mother who had a hard time of it keeping them all together. Maria watched the little ones darting in and out of the reeds. One in particular seemed to be especially adventurous and went further away from the family group than the others. She wished she'd brought some bread with her to scatter for them.

Then she saw a car approaching. It slowed down and stopped. A moment later the back door opened and Polly climbed out. She leaned inside the car for a moment to speak to the elderly couple who had driven her from home and then shut the door and waved farewell as they drove away.

'Over here, Polly!' Maria cried.

Her sister's face lit up and she ran forward to hug Maria, dropping her large shoulder bag to the ground. She looked great in the bright colours she favoured and she'd had her hair cut short in a style that suited her.

'You look wonderful,' Maria told her.

Polly's eyes sparkled. 'I'm so glad to be here. I can't wait to be back on board *Dreamcatcher.* We've missed it like anything, both of us. And I can't wait to catch up with your news, too.'

Maria smiled, seeming to catch some of her sister's glowing warmth. 'There's so much to tell you, Polly. But first, how's Neil?'

'Aching to be back on board,' said Polly with satisfaction. 'As keen as me now. Keener. They want to see him again at the hospital tomorrow, but after his appointment we'll

160

drive straight back to where I leave you tonight to give us time to race to Bemerton on Friday.'

'Race?' said Maria, laughing. 'I don't think so.'

'Chug along at a decent speed, I mean, of course,' said Polly happily, picking up her bag. 'Sorry, Maria, but it means you having to hang about all tomorrow until we can get back to you. You won't mind that, will you?'

'Not if it means you joining me in the evening.'

'That's the plan,' said Polly. 'Ready for a really early start on Friday. Bemerton here we come!'

'Come on then,' said Maria. '*Dreamcatcher* awaits.'

She had made sure that the narrowboat was looking its best by sweeping the floor and wiping the units extra clean. The well-deck had been swabbed, too, and the railings polished with a dry cloth.

*   *   *

Polly let out a breath of pure pleasure as she stepped aboard.

It took only moments to pull up the mooring pegs from the bank and stow them on deck and then they were off with Polly holding the tiller lightly in one hand.

'There's nothing like it, this gorgeous smell of grassy banks and foliage,' she said, taking

161

deep, appreciative sniffs of the morning air.

'Coffee?' said Maria from down below.

'Great idea.'

Maria's mobile rang as she was reaching the coffee jar down from the shelf. Luke with news of Charlie! Her heart thudded as she heard his familiar voice sounding, thankfully, upbeat.

'Good news, Maria,' he said. 'I've just had the vet on the phone. Charlie can be discharged today. He's getting over the trauma very well, poor old chap.'

'Thank goodness,' she breathed.

'I hope it's OK but I've asked if he can stay where he is until other arrangements can be made. They board animals at the vets so it's no problem. I hope I did right?'

Maria glanced around at the confined space. She had been so worried about Charlie's injuries that she hadn't thought much of the immediate practical details. *Dreamcatcher* was no place for an injured dog.

'Thank you, Luke,' she said humbly.

'I'll go along and check on him presently,' he said. 'Everything all right with *Dreamcatcher*? Are you on the move yet?'

'Just setting off, Polly and me.'

'Good luck then,' he said. 'See you, Maria.'

He clicked off his phone and Maria stood for a moment gazing down at hers. His voice had been full of deep concern for a dog that wasn't even his.

She remembered his admission that he

never felt inspired to paint animals in spite of his deep love for them. Scenes with water in them were the subject of his lovely paintings. The canal, of course, and the lovely moorland scene with the glimpse of distant water.

He had told her he was busy on a series of paintings for the Open Studios Event in Bemerton this weekend using acrylics so they would dry quickly. And yet he had given up his time willingly to look after Charlie.

*   *   *

'This is the life,' Polly said when Maria carried up the two mugs of coffee. She sighed a little. 'Poor old Neil left behind today. I made him promise not to do anything stupid and threatened that I wouldn't drive him down here after his hospital appointment tomorrow if he did.'

Maria smiled.

'Come on then, tell me all your news,' Polly demanded.

'Did you know that Luke is the owner of *Dreamcatcher*?' Maria asked.

Polly looked at her in amazement. 'Luke is? I don't believe it.'

'That's what he said.'

'That's incredible. Do you mean he actually owns this boat and he never said a word?'

'So you and Neil didn't know?'

'Would I have kept such an interesting item

163

of news to myself?' Polly said in indignation.

Maria laughed. 'I didn't think you would.'

'But why?' said Polly. 'I mean, why were we asked to deliver his boat to Bemerton? Sounds crazy to me.'

'There seemed to be some row about it at the wharf office in Yarnley while I was waiting for you,' Maria said. 'Luke told me he was too busy to get it to Bemerton himself. That's all I know.'

'Well, that's something to think about,' said Polly. 'So what else is new?'

So much had been happening that recounting it with frequent interruptions from her sister took Maria a long time. Polly was especially interested in Gary's reaction to Charlie's disappearance.

'So Gary just stormed off?' she said. 'I'd never have thought that even of him.'

'I would never have thought he'd turn up with a dog in the first place,' said Maria.

Polly looked curious. 'Weren't you upset when Gary went, not even the teeniest tiniest bit?'

Maria shook her head. 'Only about him leaving *Dreamcatcher* in the lurch. That was a bit of a facer. And about Charlie, of course. That was really upsetting. I didn't know what to do.'

'And Luke came at once to help you out,' Polly mused. 'Good of him to drop everything. A knight in shining armour, our Luke.'

Maria felt her face grow warm, remembering the picnic tea of fish and chips in his apartment and the kiss he had given her afterwards that had left her feeling emotionally shaken. She could still feel his lips on hers and the warmth that flowed through her body.

'So there's more to it?' said Polly, interested.

For a few moments Maria was silent, knowing that her sympathy had been entirely with Luke when his hand had connected with Gary's jaw.

At last she told Polly something of what had happened that evening, expecting triumph from her sister and for Polly to take credit for throwing Luke and her together in the first place. As her stumbling words came out, the sympathy in Polly's voice deepened but she didn't once mention her matchmaking schemes. Polly had never liked Gary but surprisingly she was obviously trying hard not to see him as the villain of the piece.

'I've never known you to be so fair to Gary, Polly,' Maria said. 'What's got into you?'

'Are you sure you don't harbour any little secret thoughts about him? You two were so close.'

'Not one single thought in that sense.'

'That's OK then. He's gone. Finished with. Now, let's get on ourselves.'

Maria pulled open the canal map and

spread it out on the breakfast bar.

'We've got two locks to negotiate today if we get that far,' she said.

Excitement flickered through her at the thought.

'Easy-peasy,' said Polly.

Maria and her sister sat side by side on the bench. The sun was warm now and it was pleasant chugging along. A couple of swans followed them for a while, and they saw a heron standing motionless on one leg on the bank. They passed several moored boats and slowed down to pass them. The may blossom was fading now and had a brown tinge where it had been pure white only a few days ago. Maria missed the showers of white petals floating on the water.

Another narrowboat was heading towards them through open gates as they approached the first lock, which meant they could steer straight in. That was easy. And it was Polly's turn to open the gates when they arrived at the second.

'So far, so good,' she said when she climbed on board again. 'We're old hands at this now, you and I, Maria. Nothing to worry about but just enjoying ourselves.'

*   *   *

They travelled peacefully along, taking turns at the tiller. At lunch time they moored beneath trees and Maria scrambled some of the eggs and made toast. There was cola to drink and apples that Polly had brought with her. They ate sitting out on the bank for a change and afterwards they took on water at a convenient water point and then tackled a swing bridge.

'So,' said Polly as the afternoon wore on. 'You really like Luke, Maria? Love him a little, even?'

'I feel shattered each time I leave him,' Maria murmured. 'Is that love?'

'And how does he feel about you?'

But that was something Maria couldn't answer.

She shrugged.

'I don't know.'

*   *   *

After a while Polly went down below to fetch the map up on deck. She was silent for a moment, studying it with her dark head bent. They had been on the move now for several hours and both girls were tired.

'A main road crosses the canal just past bridge sixty-one,' she said. 'It looks a good point to be picked up. Easy for Ted and Olive to find, too. I suggest we head there to wait for them. What d'you think?'

'Sounds good,' said Maria.

Polly took over the tiller while Maria consulted the map. The canal meandered a great deal, moving in great loops through the countryside. Bemerton was only a mile or two closer now than from where they had started this morning.

'And I see there's a convenient pub nearby for some food if there's time,' she said.

Polly pulled out her mobile. 'I promised I'd ring about this time and tell Ted and Olive where we'll be.'

'I'll take the tiller,' said Maria.

Polly made her call. 'That's OK,' she said when she clicked her phone off again. 'About an hour, Ted said. Will we do it, d'you think?'

Maria moved the lever forward a little. 'Why not if we go on like this? It's not far. Enough time for us to grab something to eat, too.'

'Perfect,' said Polly.

*   *   *

There was too much time as it turned out. They ate outside the pub at a picnic table from where they had a good view of the road and the bridge where Ted would stop the car. Cars sped by and the occasional lorry, filling the air with traffic noise and diesel fumes they weren't accustomed to.

At first, Polly, relaxed, enjoyed her scampi and chips and didn't look at her watch once. But as the evening went on and she knew the time had come and gone for her friends to appear at the meeting place, she kept jumping up to look over at the road to see if they were waiting in a spot where she couldn't see them.

'They could have got held up somewhere,' Maria pointed out.

'Don't be sensible,' Polly said. 'It doesn't help.'

'Give them a ring, why don't you?'

'No signal,' Polly said gloomily when she had tried her mobile. 'Wouldn't you just know it?'

'The pub will have a land line,' said Maria, finishing the last drop of her lemon and lime. She indicated Polly's empty glass. 'Can I get you another?'

Polly shook her head. 'I don't know their daughter's number,' she said.

'Directory enquiries?'

'I don't know her surname.' Polly drummed her fingers on the edge of the table. 'I've got to be back home tonight. How else will Neil get to the hospital tomorrow if there's no-one to drive him?' She sounded close to tears.

'Come on,' said Maria. 'Let's walk about a bit. It'll help pass the time.'

Polly sprang up and was away over the grass to the wall that overlooked the road in seconds. Maria joined her more slowly.

'Oh, where are they?' Polly moaned.

Maria looked at her sympathetically, wishing she could help. It was now over an hour since the arranged time.

'They couldn't have got held up this long. They'd have phoned.'

'You haven't got a signal,' Maria pointed out.

'They could have left a message on voice mail. Or a text.'

'You still wouldn't know.'

'We'd have been home by now if they'd come on time. Neil will be frantic.'

Maria glanced up and down the busy road. No white car among the passing vehicles.

A bus heading for Bemerton stopped and three people alighted. Maria saw there was a timetable near the bus stop sign.

'I'll go and phone Neil and tell him what's happening, shall I?' she said to Polly. 'If your neighbours arrive while I'm away, just go. I'll know you've not been kidnapped.'

Polly nodded, not even able to raise a smile. 'Don't be long.'

Neil took a long time to come to the phone and Maria was beginning to fear that something was seriously wrong, when she heard his voice at last. He sounded worried for his excitable wife.

'I'll calm her down,' Maria promised. 'I'm sorry about this, Neil.'

'Hardly your fault. I'll go round in a minute and see if Ted and Olive are home yet. They could have been involved in an accident, had you thought of that?'

'Polly hasn't. I did wonder.'

'Phone me back in half an hour, why don't you? No mobile signal where you are?'

'I'm using the phone at the pub. We're on a bus route, Neil. Polly could get to Bemerton tomorrow morning and then home from there if the worst happens and they don't show.'

She put the phone down thoughtfully and returned to *Dreamcatcher.*

*   *   *

'Why ever did we dream up this stupid project in the first place?' Polly moaned.

They were back on board, waiting for thirty minutes to pass before Maria could return to phone Neil. From here they had a good view of the bridge and Polly didn't take her eyes from it.

'You're not regretting your dream surely?' said Maria.

'All the hassle and trouble! I could do without it. It's crazy. I wish we'd never heard of canals and narrowboats.'

Maria smiled. 'You don't mean that, Polly.'

'Neil's cousin can go and jump for someone else to go into partnership with him. I want out.'

'Calm down. We'll work something out.'

'Calm down?' said Polly in indignation. 'I've never been calmer in my life. I've come to my senses, that's all. This life isn't for us and I'll tell Neil when I get back home. If I ever do.'

171

Maria got up.

'Where are you going?' Polly demanded.

'To phone Neil, remember?'

'Tell him I've had it up to here. He can phone Steve at once and tell him.'

'You'll be OK here while I'm gone, won't you?' Maria said anxiously. 'Best to stay and watch for Ted and Olive. They could turn up yet.'

The thirty minutes had been slow to pass with Polly in this depressed and angry mood. Maria was relieved that Neil's voice sounded calm and controlled when he picked up the phone.

'A misunderstanding,' he told her. 'That's all. No accident, thank goodness. I was relieved to see them turn up, I can tell you. Apparently they waited at bridge sixty-seven for three quarters of an hour and then didn't know what to do.'

'Bridge sixty-one,' said Maria.

'They know that now, and couldn't be more sorry. They left a message on Polly's mobile.'

'She hasn't received it yet,' said Maria.

'Not to worry,' said Neil. 'I'm fine here and Polly can get back by bus in the morning. No harm done. Ted's going to drive me for my appointment tomorrow, so that's OK. Get Polly to come to the phone, will you?'

'Will do,' said Maria. 'Goodnight then, Neil. See you soon.'

Before returning to *Dreamcatcher*, Maria

checked the bus times for the next morning. Now all she had to do was pacify her sister and get her to talk to Neil who, no doubt, would be able to reassure her that their future plans were not the disaster she thought they were.

JOURNEY'S END

Polly was up and dressed next morning by the time Maria emerged on deck, yawning, at 6 a.m.

'You're up early.'

'I couldn't sleep,' said Polly, white-faced.

'The first bus isn't till seven,' Maria reminded her. 'So . . . breakfast first. Cereal, toast?'

'I'm not hungry,' said Polly.

Maria turned the grill to high and sliced two pieces of bread. 'Here, take this towel and dry the seats outside. We'll eat out on deck.'

She carried the tray of food and two mugs of strong tea up the steps into the bright morning air.

'Another lovely day,' she said with satisfaction. 'Everything'll be fine, you'll see.'

Polly frowned. 'Let's hope so. Neil's determined it will be. And he's even keener than me now.'

'That's good,' said Maria. 'No, that came out wrong. You're worried, that's all. Your

173

enthusiasm will be back as soon as you get back here again with Neil. I'm sure of it, Polly. You'll be raring to go and nothing will stop you.'

Polly looked broodingly at her toast. 'I hope you're right.'

'Of course I am,' said Maria confidently.

They ate in silence. The ducklings were happy this morning with the scraps Polly threw overboard for them.

'I'll come on the bus to Bemerton with you, if you like,' said Maria as they finished the meal and she started to collect their plates together. 'To make sure you get on the right one from there.'

'Don't you trust me then?'

'In the state you're in you could end up anywhere.'

Polly shivered. 'I'd rather you stayed here and guarded *Dreamcatcher* after what you've told me about those thugs pulling up the mooring pegs,' she said.

Maria hesitated. 'OK then, maybe you've got a point. If my car was here it might be different. Relying on bus times could be a bit dodgy in this remote place. I could be away a long time.'

'I'm sure it's best to stay.'

'But Polly, don't worry,' said Maria. 'Ted and Olive are taking Neil to hospital. You've just got to get yourself home in one piece.'

Polly smiled as she gathered up her

belongings. 'Will you walk me to the bus stop, Maria? I might get lost.'

'Of course,' said Maria, smiling too, glad to hear a spark of humour in her sister's voice.

*　　　*　　　*

She made sure to lock *Dreamcatcher*'s door and then followed Polly on to the towpath.

They didn't have long to wait at the bus stop before a double-decker came lumbering round the corner and pulled up alongside them. Maria wrinkled her nose at the smell of warm diesel. Polly got on and bought her ticket and the bus moved off.

Maria was sad to see her go but she waved her sister off with a smile. Hopefully Polly would be home before too long and all would be well with Neil so she could drive them both back to Bemerton later that day.

The sky was a wispy blue now, not quite as bright as when they were eating their toast out on deck. The dewy grass that bordered the towpath wet her feet in her sandals and made the bottoms slippery. She left wet footprints on deck as she went below to change into trainers.

First she must attend to the washing-up and get everything tidied. Her bed needed making and she had left yesterday's clothes scattered on the bedroom floor. Even by working ultra slowly it was still only half-past seven when she'd finished and she had aeons of empty hours ahead of her before she could even begin to think of Polly and Neil's return.

* * *

She returned to the deck to open the trap door in the floor to check the bilge and press the button to empty any water that had seeped in during the night. She replaced the cover with a clatter that frightened away an exploring moorhen with a cry of alarm.

Where was Polly now? Hopefully boarding a bus in Bemerton to take her the rest of the way home. Maria gazed thoughtfully at the misty bank of trees on the horizon. In the distance an engine throbbed and after a while a narrowboat came into view round the bend in the canal and, slowing down, passed her. Only the faintest movement of the water disturbed *Dreamcatcher* at her mooring. Luke would approve of that, she thought. But some water lily leaves and one yellow flower over on the other side of the canal decided not to risk anything and disappeared beneath the surface until danger had passed.

The man at the tiller waved. 'Lovely morning,' he said.

'Great,' she responded.

She watched until he was out of sight and then went below to bring the canal map up with her. Moving *Dreamcatcher* to the next bridge might be a good idea. Or somewhere

176

further on with a good mobile signal.

*   *   *

Polly leaned back in her bus seat, glad to be doing something positive. Maria had the worst of it, stuck there in *Dreamcatcher* for hours on end not knowing what was going on. She still felt sore about Ted and Olive, sure that she had told them the correct bridge number. But at least they were doing their best to make amends by driving Neil to hospital and hopefully staying with him until he'd seen the doctor. They could then drive him home again if she didn't manage to get to the hospital in time to drive him home herself.

And the sun was shining. Great. She gazed out of the bus window at fields and hedgerows. Not even the grimy glass could dull the scene on this bright morning.

They were arriving in Bemerton now, driving up the busy High Street on the way to the bus station. As she got off she made enquiries about the bus she needed to take her home.

'Ask at the office, love,' she was told.

In contrast to the quietness of the canal the noise here was terrific, even at this early hour. Car horns tooted, doors slammed and jostling people called to one another.

To her dismay, the bus she needed didn't leave for another hour and then would take a

177

roundabout route adding time to the journey. But there was no choice, take the bus and be a long time getting home or stay there.

She was reminded of their arrival at Yarnley Wharf all those days ago and of having to wait for Luke to attend to them before they could set off in *Dreamcatcher*. And there he was now, if her eyes didn't deceive her, striding across the road in her direction.

'Luke!' she called.

He stopped short and then a smile lit his face as he saw her. She smiled back. He really was handsome with that fair hair and a blue shin that highlighted the colour of his eyes.

'Polly, by all that's wonderful. What are you doing here?'

She told him, playing down Ted and Olive's part in her predicament.

'So Maria's alone on *Dreamcatcher*?'

'Waiting there till we get back tonight.'

He frowned. 'She won't try to get to Bemerton today in *Dreamcatcher* on her own, will she?'

'You haven't a high opinion of my sister, have you?'

'The company won't think highly of her if she does. It's a condition of hiring out boats that the hirers have to have the right number of crew on board. You know that.'

Polly did. She also knew that Maria had once before moved the boat on her own. She bit her lip.

178

'Don't forget this is a test for you and Neil and your crew. It's important to be considered reliable. You don't want to foul up now the end is in sight.'

Polly hesitated. 'I can't phone Maria and warn her,' she said. 'There's no mobile signal at bridge sixty-one.'

'Have I your permission to act as your representative and move *Dreamcatcher* with Maria?' he asked.

'Yes! Oh yes.'

'I'll leave my car in the pub car park there. They know it well. It means us having to get all the way to Bemerton though. You might wish to do the last miles yourself, of course, but there would be difficulty in me getting back to my vehicle if we don't go the whole way.'

Polly thought carefully. Luke's kind suggestion would be far the best thing for Maria. No hanging around all day waiting until she and Neil appeared. There was no guarantee, after all, that they would manage it this evening. In any case they could be very late getting back.

'Brilliant,' she said at last. Maria had been so good to them, so supportive. For Maria's sake she would be glad to forgo the euphoria of being on board *Dreamcatcher* for the last few miles.

Luke looked at her closely. 'You're quite sure?'

'Positive,' Polly said. 'If all goes well we'll

see you back in Bemerton late this evening.'

She fished in her bag for pad and biro.

'What are you doing?'

'Making it all above board,' she said, scribbling hastily. She tore off the paper and handed it to him. 'Your official permission, signed by me,' she said.

'My, aren't we efficient?'

She smiled. 'Someone's got to be and I might as well start as I mean to go on.'

Laughing, he took the paper from her. 'I'd better get a move on before Maria decides to go it alone,' he said.

'Good luck.'

He flashed a brilliant smile and was gone.

*　　　*　　　*

Maria glanced up at the sky. Those wispy clouds had moved away now and the warmth from the early sunshine was pleasant on her face. She checked that the mooring pegs were still in place. No problem there. Then she went down the steps for the book she had left in the bedroom, and heard Luke's voice calling from somewhere near.

She was imagining things now. Smiling at her fancies she returned to the deck and saw him on the bank with the sunlight on his fair hair.

'Hi there, Maria.'

She stared at him in astonishment. 'What

are you doing here?'

'Come to help,' he said. 'Can I come aboard?'

Without waiting for an answer he stepped on to the deck and smiled at her.

'So you're stuck here at the moment,' he said. 'Since you can't move *Dreamcatcher* on your own, according to contract, I'd better give you a hand.'

'There's no need, Luke, really. I know how busy you are with the art weekend. We've got it all under control. Polly and Neil will be coming back.'

'That's risky. They might not get back in time. What then?'

'I'll manage.'

'You won't on your own.'

'So you think I can't cope? It's only a few miles to Bemerton.'

'That's not the point. I won't allow it.'

'So . . . who are you to stop me?'

'*Dreamcatcher*'s owner,' he said.

'Pulling rank?' she said. 'That's not fair.'

He smiled disarmingly at her. 'Of course it isn't. Who said life was fair?'

She was still astonished at him being there. 'You'll really help me to get *Dreamcatcher* to Bemerton?'

'Why not? You'll find I know how to handle a narrowboat quite well with a bit of help from you.'

A laugh caught in her throat and she looked

at him in wonder. He was serious about helping her!

'Polly's expecting me to stay moored here.'

'I saw Polly in Bemerton. There's not a bus for ages. She's given her permission for me to help you get *Dreamcatcher* all the way to the marina.'

'You needed my sister's permission to move your own boat?'

He looked at her with a smile on his lips but a serious expression in his eyes. 'I do for the terms of the contract.'

She felt the warmth flood her face and looked away from him. He moved slightly beside her. 'Have you checked the grease?'

She smiled. 'And emptied the bilge.'

'Good girl.'

She raised her eyes to look at him. He looked so strong and capable as he gazed back at her that her heart was stirred.

'Your sister and brother-in-law will be meeting us at Bemerton Marina,' he said. 'Tomorrow if not tonight.'

He pulled out the piece of paper Polly had given him. 'Here are my credentials. I hope they pass muster.'

She nodded, smiling. 'Except that my sister's handwriting is very hard to read.'

'Then you'll have to take me on trust,' he said, sounding purposeful now. 'We'd better get moving, don't you think?'

'You're right. Let's go.'

The engine sprang to life as he turned the key. She leapt on to the bank to deal with the ropes and mooring pegs. Back on board again she gave a huge sigh of happiness. The warmth that flowed through her as she stood beside him was not only from the effort of pulling the pegs from the bank.

Luke was there to help her! There was no doubt, now, that *Dreamcatcher* would get where she needed to be with plenty of time to spare.

*   *   *

Dreamcatcher's engine seemed to know that Luke was in charge, Maria thought, because it seemed quieter, more content as they moved steadily past banks of long grass and wild flowers. She saw red campion and vetch and the occasional yellow wild iris standing sentinel at the edge.

'What are you smiling at?' asked Luke.

'Just foolish fancies,' she said. 'I love seeing the water lilies fold up and disappear under the water as we approach.'

'I've never seen so many of their yellow flowers as I have this year,' Luke commented.

His tanned hand was resting lightly on the tiller as they sat together on the seat. The afternoon was a haven of beauty and she felt privileged to be part of it.

Soon they came to a belt of trees. The

countryside was changing and there were hills now where earlier the land had been flat. But still the peace prevailed.

She made coffee and sandwiches but they didn't moor to eat their lunch. They were too anxious to get to their destination and yet at the same time Maria wished they could go on for ever.

*   *   *

Much later, as the afternoon was slipping into evening, Maria brought *Dreamcatcher* into the marina at Bemerton and heard Luke's murmur of approval as he jumped ashore with the mooring ropes. The joy of bringing the narrowboat gently into the bank and knowing she had done what they had set out to do was almost more than she could bear.

Luke made the ropes fast to the mooring rings and then came back on board.

'All done,' he said, smiling at her.

She sank down on the seat, surprisingly tired. 'Thank you, Luke. You've been great.'

A slight commotion over by the café attracted her attention and she saw Polly before Polly saw her.

'We're here!' Maria cried, waving at her.

'Maria!' The expression on Polly's face was a mixture of delight and anxiety.

Maria felt a thud of fear as Polly joined them. 'Isn't Neil with you? How is he?'

'He's talking to the chap in the office,' said Polly. 'He's all right. His injury is healing nicely.'

'And *Dreamcatcher* is delivered safe and sound,' said Maria. She jumped ashore and ran to her sister to give her a hug. 'Oh, Polly, it's great to see you.'

Polly was highly delighted too, jumping up and down. 'Wonderful,' she cried. 'I'm so glad to see you, too, Luke. Thank you for everything.'

He grinned at her, pleased at her reaction. But he wasn't hanging about. With a casual wave he disappeared towards the office. Maria watched his fair head above the crowd of people until she could see it no more.

'I thought I saw Gary just now,' said Polly, perplexed. 'Is he still around in Bemerton, do you know?'

'Could be,' said Maria.

'Neil wants a word with him,' Polly said. 'We owe Gary a debt of gratitude, don't forget.'

Maria hadn't forgotten that Gary had given up part of his holiday to help them. She would have to see him again and thank him. And there was still the matter of Charlie to sort out once and for all.

Her sister's smile was so wide as she looked about her that it was catching. Maria smiled too, though she had a strange feeling of anticlimax now the job was done. She'd had a great time on board in spite of everything, but

185

now all that was left was for her to go home and get on with her life there.

But first there was Charlie to think about and visit and, if she decided she couldn't keep him, find a good home.

'I'm so grateful to you, Maria,' Polly said enthusiastically as she went from one end of the boat to the other. 'Hopefully all is in order but it's not signed on the bottom line yet. We'll know soon, with luck. Tomorrow, anyway. Come back to the office with me and find Neil and we'll celebrate.'

Maria smiled at her. She had done the best she could to help Polly realise her dream and in doing so she had discovered things about herself. One of them was that she loved the life of the inland waterways. Maybe she would come again on holiday when the business was up and running.

'It's you and Neil who need to celebrate . . . together,' she said. 'If you're sure it's not too soon. I'm going to have a look round the place first. I'll join you later.'

PARTY TIME!

Club Sonek was moored further along the bank hidden by the branches of a willow tree that hung over its roof. No one was on board that Maria could see. Had Gary gone off home already leaving Charlie behind?

When Gary had first arrived with Charlie he had said he was looking for a home for the dog. Now she must sort out what was going to happen to him.

She found Gary seated at one of the tables outside *The Noisy Duck*, the small café set back from the waterside. He appeared to be alone. His cup of coffee was less than half full and he was staring into space, the corners of his mouth downcast. He looked so lonely that she felt a rush of sympathy for him.

'Gary?'

His sad expression didn't change as he looked up and saw her. 'Hi, Maria. I wasn't expecting to see you. You got here then?'

'*Dreamcatcher*'s moored further along,' she said. 'I didn't see *Club Sonek* at first. Are you all right, Gary?'

'I'm sorry I sloped off like that. It was out of order but I'd had it up to here with that dog. I couldn't take any more.'

'I found him soon after you'd left,' she said. 'He wasn't far away. He'd been hit by a car.'

'On the towpath? You're joking.'

'On the road,' said Maria, biting her lip. 'He must have gone wandering up there.'

'Stupid dog. Pity it didn't finish him off.'

'You don't mean that, Gary.'

'Of course I mean it. He's been nothing but trouble.'

'We got him to the vet. He's going to be all

187

right. I thought you would want to know that.'
She could hardly believe his lack of concern.

He shrugged. 'It's something I could do without, I can tell you that. He should have been put down while you had the chance.'

'I simply don't understand how you came to offer to look after Charlie in the first place.'

'I told you,' he said. 'To do a friend a good turn.'

Maria sat down on the spare seat at his table. 'But you don't like animals, dogs especially,' she said patiently. Gary had tried to do her a good turn, too. She mustn't forget that.

'So where's the dog now?' he asked, picking up his cup and downing the rest of his coffee.

'He's still at the vet's. He's going to be all right, thank goodness.'

'You said *we* just now? Who's we?'

'Luke's his name. He came to give me a hand as you weren't there.'

'You don't mean that thug who goes around with an easel and board?' He rubbed his jaw as if it was still painful. 'He'd better have the good sense to keep out of my way in future.'

Maria flushed. 'Luke's an artist, yes,' she said. 'A good one.' It wouldn't do to get into an argument with Gary now. It was Charlie's welfare they needed to discuss.

But Gary still showed an annoying lack of concern. 'The dog's owners have gone abroad, I told you that,' he said. 'No good expecting

188

them to cough up for vet's fees. I'm supposed to be getting rid of the wretched animal for them anyway.'

'I'll take him,' said Maria swiftly, surprising herself. She took a deep breath. Now what had she done? Polly was the impulsive one, not her. But she knew this decision was the right one and she wasn't about to go back on it. She would work something out.

'I'll pay the vet's bill in lieu of payment for Charlie.'

'If you like. It'll solve a problem for me.'

As easy as that and she was a dog owner! And not any old dog either. A very special dog. She loved Charlie and now he was hers. But she needed to make everything above board with no fear of any come-back in the future. Maria smiled.

'We need paper and a biro,' she said, remembering the joke permission form that Luke had produced. 'I've got some back at the boat. Hold on and wait here. You can write me out some sort of receipt and we'll both sign it.'

'I'll get the coffees in,' said Gary, standing up.

'I won't be long,' she said.

She ran back to *Dreamcatcher*, explained hurriedly to Polly and Neil what she was doing and left them speechless at the speed she was on and off the boat. She wanted to make sure that Gary didn't take it into his head not to wait at *The Noisy Duck* after all.

*   *   *

He had got a plate of doughnuts as well as the coffee. Maria found she was hungry and ate two hurriedly as Gary took the paper and pen from her.

'What have you put?' she asked as he finished.

They bent over the paper together and Maria saw that he had written words to the effect that she was the owner of Charlie from this date and that any bills accrued would be paid by her.

'Simple enough, but effective,' he said with satisfaction. 'And I wish you joy of the brute.'

He sounded complacent and she looked at him in confusion. How had she loved this man enough to consider spending the rest of her life with him? This seemed incredible to her now but it was all in the past and she had come to her senses in time.

'And the dog is still at the vet's you say?' Gary asked.

'He's boarding at the veterinary practice here in Bemerton. He's happy there for the time being.'

'No doubt living in the lap of luxury. How much is that going to cost? Have you thought of that?'

'He's worth it.' She smiled and raised her face, feeling excited now and happy that she

190

wouldn't have to give Charlie up to anyone.

'So, where's Bella?' she asked.

'She had something to attend to at the marina office,' Gary told her, handing over the receipt for Charlie. 'She said she'd meet me here after she'd seen that artist bloke, Luke. Wouldn't tell me why she's meeting him. There's no accounting for tastes. She'll be along in a minute.'

'Then I'd better not stay here any longer,' said Maria, pocketing the precious piece of paper and standing up.

Gary looked alarmed. 'Don't go, Maria. We've got to talk.'

'Bella can have my coffee. I haven't touched it.'

He got up too and she thought he would try to restrain her. Instead he stood looking down at her, a serious expression on his face.

'I'm prepared to forget about the row earlier,' he said. 'Can't we make a go of it, my love? That's what I hoped when I got your phone call asking for my help on the narrowboat.'

'I'm sorry, Gary,' she said firmly.

'I know you don't always see eye to eye with me but surely we can overcome that? We were good together once. Have you forgotten that?'

'We lost it. I know that now for sure. You were right at the time about wanting to finish.'

'But not any more. I need you in my life, Maria.'

'I'll be grateful to you as long as I live for what you've done for us this week even if it ended badly with Charlie's disappearance.'

'That dog again,' he said with scorn.

'That dog means a lot to me,' she said quietly.

He shrugged. 'You've made that crystal clear.'

'So now it's goodbye.'

'Are you going to the get-together in the marina building tonight?'

She hesitated. 'Maybe. And you? Are you going to it with Bella?'

'Bella!' He said the girl's name with the same disdain he'd had in his voice when he'd been talking about Charlie earlier.

'Here she is now,' said Maria as she caught sight of the dark-haired girl coming towards them. 'I can't stay, Gary. Believe me it's over between us. I hope that one day you'll meet the right person and be happy.'

With a hasty wave to Bella she was off, darting round the corner between *The Noisy Duck* and the chandler's shop. Things seemed to be over between Gary and Bella, too, if she'd read the signs correctly, she thought. She felt a stab of disappointment for him.

It would have been such a satisfactory ending to the week from her point of view, knowing that Gary's good turn to her was repaid with a new and happier relationship for himself. But it was not to be. The charming

Bella had been friendly towards him, that was all, as she probably was with everyone.

It was strange though that both Bella and Luke had important business matters to attend to at the same time at the marina office.

*   *   *

Visiting Charlie was her next priority but it was late now and she'd have to wait until tomorrow. Maria, her thoughts on her dog, wandered back to *Dreamcatcher.* The narrowboat lay at its moorings looking peaceful and unconcerned. The sky was cloudy now, casting a dismal atmosphere over the scene.

She found Polly rummaging through a pile of clothes on the bed in the end bedroom. Polly and Neil would be sleeping there tonight after the party.

'Where's Neil?' she asked her sister.

Polly looked round at her. 'Gone off somewhere to clear his head. Can't keep still and neither can I. Oh, Maria, this business means so much to us.'

Maria seated herself on the corner of the bed.

'I know,' she said sympathetically. 'But you've got to relax.'

She was glad to see Polly's smile. It soon vanished again though, as she flopped down on her back beside Maria and gave a huge

193

stretch.

'There,' she said. 'Totally relaxed and able to deal with anything.'

'With a coiled spring inside,' said Maria. 'Like me.'

Polly sat up and grabbed Maria in a hug, then let her go again. She took several large breaths. 'We're fools, the pair of us,' she said. 'Come on, help me choose what to wear this evening.'

By the time they had settled on dark jeans and a clover-coloured top that suited Polly's dark looks, Neil was back. Maria had kept a new pair of jeans for herself, tucked safely away at the back of the cupboard, as well as a pretty flowered top and strappy sandals that made her feel good.

She thought of Luke as she put them on, remembering his scorn at her worn trainers that first day. Soon she would be seeing him again, dressed for once in something she knew looked good.

She smiled at herself in the mirror as she combed her hair and slipped on some sparkly earrings.

*   *   *

Lively music filled the air as the three of them approached the empty warehouse where the party was being held.

Polly clutched at Maria's arm. 'Are you

194

ready for this? I'm not sure I am.'

As they went in, Maria saw that someone had spent time decorating the walls with huge dark fishing nets and colourful spinnakers from sailing dinghies to hide the brickwork. Gary would feel at home, she thought. She looked round for him among the crowd of people but couldn't see him.

They moved towards the drinks table and added their own contribution. Then, with full glasses in their hands, they mingled with the other guests, exchanging pleasantries and tales of exploits at locks and in tunnels. There was food too, but Maria wasn't hungry. She could see from Polly's look of dismay as she glanced at it that she wasn't either and neither was Neil.

'I can't see Luke anywhere,' said Polly.

'Nor me,' said Maria. She had expected to see his fair head above the others, moving in their direction. Disappointment coursed through her like the current on a busy river. She stood back against the wall as a young boy tapped Polly on the shoulder.

'You're needed in the office,' he said, looking at Neil too.

'This is it at last,' Polly whispered to Maria. 'The go-ahead or not to join in with the narrowboat hiring business.'

Neil took his wife's arm with his uninjured one. 'Come on, love,' he said. He looked more purposeful now than Maria had ever seen him.

'Good luck!' she called as they left her to follow the boy through the throng. She sent up a silent prayer as she moved to the end of the room to wait for them to come back. She looked round for somewhere to place her empty glass and put it down on a handy box.

Even though she was surrounded by partying people she now felt lonelier than she had ever felt in her life. Suddenly the music seemed to rise to such a crescendo she couldn't bear it. She pushed her way to the door and out into the calm evening air.

Out here there was no one. She walked a little way and stood looking at the narrowboats tied up to the metal jetties. They were all deserted because their crews were enjoying themselves inside the lighted building she had just left. The pulsing music from behind her faded as she moved further away to sit at one of the picnic benches on the canal bank.

Why hadn't Luke been at the party? Or Bella?

*   *   *

Dusk was falling now, the sounds around her muted. She heard a small splash and a drowsy squawk. She liked the peace after the lively racket inside the warehouse. Was Charlie sleeping now, recovering from his injuries? She would visit him tomorrow. And then what? She tried to imagine herself driving back to her flat with her dog on the back seat and couldn't because it was the life here that seemed real to her now, her old life seemed a million miles away.

She sighed and then froze when she heard nearby the sound of clattering and muffled obscenities followed by the sound of a narrowboat's door sliding open. She leapt up, her heart hammering. Something was wrong. In the normal way she would have heard the crew approaching, talking about the party and laughing. But there had been nothing. Someone creeping up, taking advantage of everyone being elsewhere? She listened. No sound now, no electric light inside the nearby boat. Definitely intruders.

She turned and ran, bursting in on the festivities in the warehouse and shouting her fears with such determination that in seconds people were streaming out, using mobiles and running for their boats.

A vehicle started up and roared off. Too late to catch whoever it was who had broken into the narrowboat that had been berthed not far from *Dreamcatcher* but not too late to prevent any pilfering or damage.

Angry voices filled the air, torchlights flashed. Maria, relieved that *Dreamcatcher* hadn't been tampered with, was unable to go on board because Neil had the key with him. She went to look for him and Polly.

She found them at the door of the

warehouse, blinking bemusedly at all the activity going on outside. Polly's eyes were shining.

'What's going on?' said Neil. 'A break-in on one of the boats? Not *Dreamcatcher*?'

'They got away,' said Maria. 'But no, they didn't break into *Dreamcatcher*, Neil. And no harm done.'

'Oh, Maria, it's going to be all right,' Polly cried. 'I'll tell you when all this has died down.'

A few people returned to the warehouse to clear up and dispose of the left-over food and drink but by the time the police came to take statements the marina had quietened down and the warehouse was in darkness.

* * *

Later, seated at the table inside *Dreamcatcher* in an atmosphere charged with elation, Maria looked at Polly and Neil in wonder.

'So it's really going to be all right for you both?' she said.

Polly's smile was huge. 'Luke'll be here in a minute. He wanted to know where you were.'

'Luke?'

Neil was smiling too. He got up. 'I'll make coffee.'

'With one hand?' said Maria.

'Just watch me,' he said.

And so she watched Neil carry four mugs of coffee in turn from the galley to the table without offering to help. And then Luke arrived and sat down next to her on the narrow seat.

'Congratulations, Polly and Neil,' he said. 'I couldn't be more pleased.'

'And to think I believed in the beginning that you wanted us to make a mess of things, Luke,' Maria said, full of shame for the way she had judged him.

She wished she could talk to him in private and tell him how good Polly and Neil would be at their new jobs and that Neil wouldn't make the same mistake at the locks twice. But obviously Luke must have worked that out for himself. She felt a rush of gratitude that her sister and Neil were appreciated.

'I tried to tell her,' said Polly, laughing.

His eyes narrowed. 'Tell her what?'

'That you were a decent bloke and not a spy at all.'

'Is that what you thought, Maria?'

'Stop it, Polly,' she said.

'Yes, stop it, Polly, before you say too much,' said Neil.

'But I don't understand why you didn't seem to want us to set off on *Dreamcatcher* in the first place,' said Maria.

'I'm ashamed to say we were warned about these dreadful people, the Rankins,' said Luke. 'I admit it. I believed what I was told. Someone I trusted, you see. Her brother, actually.'

'*Club Sonek*,' said Maria quietly.

Luke smiled at Polly disarmingly. 'But I soon changed my mind about you. Am I forgiven?'

'I could forgive anybody tonight,' said Polly.

'We were interrupted back there in the office,' Neil said. 'There are still contracts to be worked out and signed. But that has to be done tomorrow, at the solicitor's, first thing.'

'And Maria?' Luke said. 'Will you be there, too?'

She hesitated, unsure of what he meant. 'I've things to do,' she said. 'Charlie to check on.'

'Of course.' He stood up. 'I'll leave you three to it now.'

The place seemed empty when he had gone. Polly and Neil suddenly set upon a plateful of bread and cheese as if they hadn't eaten for months.

Thoughtfully, Maria accepted some too and all three of them soon decided it was time for bed.

LOOSE ENDS

Maria woke early next day and lay for a moment savouring the knowledge that it wouldn't be long now before Polly and Neil's dream became reality. Everything was in place and all they had to do was get themselves along to the solicitor's office by eleven o'clock.

There they would sign the contract in the absence of Neil's cousin, Steve, who was still in New Zealand and who had arranged for a proxy to sign on his behalf. The person who had agreed to stand-in on Steve's behalf was interested in joining the business too, and was someone who was good on the practical side of things which would free Neil to attend to the finances.

'So do you think you'll get on with this other person who's going to be working with you?' Maria had asked her sister the previous evening.

Polly had smiled. 'I can't think of anyone better,' she'd said. 'He's fantastic, hard-working, kind, good-looking and very excited about it all.'

'He sounds perfect.'

'Oh, he is,' Polly had said fervently.

'But remember, any matchmaking is definitely out,' Maria had said.

'Now would I do a thing like that? I wouldn't dare.' Polly had laughed, obviously happy about it all.

'Part-owners of Roselyn Hiring,' Maria said out loud now, just to hear how it sounded. 'Well done, Polly and Neil.'

She got out of bed and got ready to face the day, pulling on the same jeans she had been wearing last night, and a clean shirt. Low-heeled sandals completed her outfit. Carefully

201

she unlocked the outside door and pushed it open, pleased that it gave only a quiet squeak.

Dawn was coming on quickly now, darkness dissolving across the canal. She'd brought a towel up with her and wiped the dew from the seat so she could sit and let the peace and beauty of the early morning wash over her. She would remember this moment for the rest of her life.

When at last Polly got up, Maria was ready to go below and help with the breakfast things. It was still early and Neil wasn't awake yet.

Polly glanced at her watch. 'I can't believe the time's going so slowly,' she said when everything they needed was on the breakfast bar. 'I simply can't wait for eleven o'clock.'

She went up on deck. 'What a glorious day. Oh look, Maria! A kingfisher.'

Maria was just in time to see a flash of blue.

'I'll make a wish,' said Polly.

'No prizes for guessing what that will be,' said Maria, laughing.

Polly looked at her, an enigmatic expression on her face. 'I don't know about that. You might be surprised at what I wished for.'

Polly moved to one side of *Dreamcatcher* and looked over at the still water. Then she moved across to the other side and back again.

Her impatience was catching and Maria found it hard to sit still herself.

'Make sure you're there too when we sign the contract, won't you?'

'Maria?' Polly said. 'You've been so much part of all this. I want you to be with us for our big moment.'

'You can count on me,' said Maria.

Polly paused in her pacing. She looked serious. 'I can always count on you.'

'Just as I have always been able to count on you ever since Mum and Dad died,' Maria said. 'Long, long years, Polly, and you've always been there for me. I've been so glad to help you now, you've no idea. Just a small thank you for your years of care . . .' She broke off, her lips trembling.

Polly looked emotional, too. Then she gave a shaky laugh and the spell was broken. They had never talked so seriously before. Maria felt relieved, somehow, as if a weight had been lifted from her.

'We've got a lot of things to talk about once this contract is signed,' Polly said happily. 'I'd better wake Neil. He's so slow with his arm in plaster he needs plenty of time to get organised.'

They made breakfast last as long as they could, each having two pieces of toast as well as bowls of cereal.

When at last the three of them locked the door of *Dreamcatcher* behind them, Polly was in a state of high excitement. 'We're going to have a look round Bemerton first,' she said.

'To use up some of the time,' said Neil. He looked as excited about it all as Polly, his

203

earlier doubts now vanished altogether. He was a new man with a purpose. It suited him, Maria thought.

'Coming with us, Maria?' asked Polly.

'I think I'll visit Charlie,' she said.

Polly's eyes danced. 'Tell him his aunt and uncle can't wait to see him.'

'Will do.'

Maria set off to walk the short distance to the veterinary practice, confident on this sunny morning that she would find Charlie a lot better and glad to see her. She hoped he hadn't forgotten her in the time he had been away.

*   *   *

Charlie's barks of welcome filled the small room where he was being accommodated. Immediately, Maria was down on her knees, trying to cradle him in her arms but not succeeding because of his frantic excitement. His right foreleg was bound in a splint but it didn't prevent him from wriggling his body about to show his deep pleasure at seeing her.

'We belong together, you and I, from now on,' Maria told him, her voice trembling with emotion. 'Did you hear that, Charlie? You're all mine now. We'll look after each other, won't we? Walks by the river every day and plenty of love around. You'll be in clover.'

She laughed as he licked her face.

It was hard to leave him, and she was unable to get the expression in his soulful eyes out of her mind for some time.

'Poor Charlie,' she murmured as she closed the door behind her. 'I'll be back soon, promise.'

*   *   *

She returned to the marina. *Dreamcatcher* was still and silent. A few ducks had gathered in the water close by and swam towards her until they realised she had nothing for them.

'Better luck next time,' she said, smiling.

Later, she found her way back to Luke's studio behind the buildings that faced the wharf. The notice on the window announced that the opening time for the Open Studios Event was two o'clock that afternoon and would run until Sunday evening. She was lucky to find the place open now, she thought.

The entrance was low and she had to bend to get through it but once inside she found another notice posted on the inside of the door. She was in a large airy room full of canvasses and all the paraphernalia of an artist's life. She sniffed at the slight smell of turpentine. The walls held many paintings, some unframed as if they were there only temporarily for the artist to stand back from them to study the effect.

Maybe that was the idea of an Open Studios

Event, she thought, to make it look as if the artist was just pausing in his work to show you round his space. Making prospective clients feel special was a good marketing tool.

There was no one else there but her.

She had seen the paintings on each of the walls as soon as she'd come in. Bright canal scenes in a mass of colours signed with the artist's name, Lucas Slane. She had loved the work of Lucas Slane in the café at the wharf in Yarnley that very first afternoon.

Luke was a hard-working artist, working all the hours he could. No time for spying for that other company! She wondered that she had ever thought so. She had a sudden sharp vision of Luke's tall figure working at his easel, totally engrossed. Painting was an important part of his life . . . such an obvious fact that she hadn't even realised it.

A thrill ran through her as she looked at the painting on the wall nearest her. Luke's hand had painted this . . . she was seeing the scene through his eyes, feeling the same emotions as he had as he'd painted it. The tunnel entrance in the painting seemed to promise some deep mystery even though he'd chosen to show it in orange and magenta. It worked. She knew exactly what he must have been feeling as he applied the paint to his canvas and then stood back to see the scene he had created.

She wandered round the room looking at the work, enjoying being in a place so close to

206

Luke's heart.

A canvas on an easel by the window pulled her up short. Luke's love of brilliant colours had been subdued a little in this beautiful painting of a girl on board a narrowboat. The setting sun cast a golden light over the smooth water. The girl's face was turned away but the pensive slope of the shoulders portrayed her personality with such sensitivity that Maria gazed at it in awe.

The doorway darkened and Luke came into the studio and stood silently at her side. She felt the warmth and vitality of him and could hardly bear it.

'I'm sorry,' she said faintly. 'I shouldn't be here.'

'Why not?'

She indicated the poster on the door as if she thought he wasn't aware of the wording on it. 'You don't open until two o'clock.'

'So?' he said, his voice husky.

'This painting's good,' she said. 'Is it for sale?' She turned to look at him and saw an expression in his eyes she hadn't seen there before.

'This one isn't for sale,' he said. 'It's mine for life as I hope one day the subject herself will be.'

She dare not think what he meant and said nothing.

'So what happened to Sir Galahad?' he asked.

'Gary?'

'The same. Has he started hounding you again?'

'He's in the past . . . where he's been for a long time.'

'Will you see him again?'

She shook her head. 'Does it matter?'

'Not a bit,' he said.

He threw back his head to look up at the clock on the wall. 'I have an appointment at eleven.'

'Me too.'

She looked at him in surprise, everything clicking into place with a suddenness that left her reeling. Today he wore a light grey jacket and trousers to match. His white shirt was open at the neck.

'At the solicitor's?' she queried.

He looked at her and smiled. 'Yes. Polly knew yesterday evening. I asked her not to mention it to you because I wanted to tell you myself.'

'But Polly can't keep secrets!'

'Maybe you don't know your sister as well as you thought you did,' he said, a teasing note in his voice.

Maybe she didn't know Luke either. He was full of surprises. She opened her mouth to say so and then shut it again. There was so much to discover about Luke. She needed time . . . years and years of it.

He nodded towards the easel. 'Do you

recognise yourself and *Dreamcatcher*, Maria?'

'Me?'

'My dearest girl, who else would it be?'

Unbelievable happiness flowed through her. She was silent, unable to form any words that could express her feelings. She turned towards him in wonder.

'I'm glad you came here this morning, Maria,' he said. 'I wanted to show my studio to you before anyone else came to see the exhibition.'

'I went to see Charlie,' she said.

'I should have included him in the painting, too, shouldn't I? But only one person is important here.' He looked at the clock again. 'And this meeting is important for both of us,' he said. 'I'll lock the studio behind me this time.'

They walked side by side through the bright morning to the solicitor's office in the High Street. There must have been traffic noise but Maria didn't hear it. There would have been people too but she was unaware of anyone except Luke and herself.

*   *   *

Maria blinked as they went into the dim building and saw the girl sitting behind the receptionist's desk.

'Hello!' she said in surprise.

Luke looked from one to the other. 'You've

met Rosie, Maria?'

'Oh yes,' said Maria, delighted to see her. She couldn't see the girl's skirt today but it probably wasn't the short yellow one she had been wearing when she'd been at the tiller of *Topsy Rose.*

'You made it to Bemerton then,' said Rosie, looking pleased. 'We went on for a few miles and then turned back. I didn't get to the party last night so I wasn't sure. Where's your sister?'

'Isn't she here yet?' said Maria in alarm.

'We're early,' said Luke.

'Take a seat, both of you,' said Rosie. 'Mr Brandon's got a client with him at the moment but he won't be long.'

'History repeating itself?' Luke muttered as they did as she said.

'They'll be here on time,' said Maria with confidence.

'I believe you,' said Luke.

He picked up the glossy magazine, *Narrowboating,* from the table in front of them and flicked it open.

'Come on then, tell me, Maria,' he said. 'Where did you and Rosie meet?'

The girls smiled at each other.

'Let's just say we had a close encounter,' said Rosie, dimpling at him.

'You could say that,' said Maria. 'I think it was our fault.'

'Six of one and half a dozen of the other,'

said Rosie, not looking at all perturbed. 'I hope Luke didn't give you grief over it.'

'Now would I do a thing like that,' he said, shutting the magazine and replacing it on the table.

Rosie winked at Maria. 'I've seen you in a tizzy once or twice, Luke, about your precious boat,' she said. 'Your brother . . .'

'Mark and I have always squabbled,' said Luke, smiling. 'I didn't want him to let Polly and Neil deliver *Dreamcatcher* for me because I had someone else in mind, but he insisted.'

'Not Bella's brother and Sonya?' said Rosie with interest.

'I'm afraid so. My mistake.'

'Have you told your brother so?'

Luke grinned. 'Mark and I are good friends again, especially as we won't be working together now I'm coming in with Roselyn Hiring. This is part of my life from now on.'

There was a commotion at the door and Polly and Neil came in. 'We're not late, are we?' said Polly.

'Stop fussing,' said Neil.

Maria saw that her sister was wearing a new outfit and that the white jeans and red shirt looked good on her. Neil, too, had changed into a white T-shirt that had obviously been recently purchased. They hadn't wasted their time, Maria thought, in preparing for their big moment.

'That's it then,' Mr Brandon said, smiling benignly at them all. He was a tall man, slightly overweight, and his rugged face looked kind. He smiled as Polly leapt from her seat to hug Neil and then Luke.

'Roselyn Hiring,' said Polly proudly. 'That's us, part-owners of a narrowboat hiring company with its own building at the marina.'

'Not to mention the house adjoining it,' said Neil.

'And no worries about security from now on as we'll make sure a security guard is on duty at all time,' said Luke. 'Bemerton Marina will be as safe as houses.'

Polly gave a sigh of pure pleasure. 'It's all systems go from now on. Our house to put on the market, the office here to sort out, the . . .'

'Hold on, Polly,' said Neil. 'There's something important for us to do first. We'll need a first-class secretary in due course. I wonder if there's anyone suitable around who would like that job?'

There was a second's silence and then Polly rushed to Maria and enveloped her in a big hug. 'You're my favourite sister in all the world,' she said.

'I think she knows that. So are you going to offer her the job?' asked Luke, laughing.

*　　　*　　　*

Afterwards, Luke took Maria to a small café he knew further along the towpath, overlooking the canal, where they could sit outside in the sunshine.

'They're not going to miss us back there,' he said. 'I've promised to reappear later to go over a few things but this time is our own. Hungry, Maria? What shall we have?'

Maria took a deep breath and then sighed happily. 'Just something long and cold to drink, please.'

He went to order and came back with two tall glasses of lime and lemonade.

'I want to show you my new apartment this afternoon,' he said. 'It's on the opposite side of the marina. Further to walk to work in my studio, of course. But I'm prepared to make sacrifices.'

'But why do you want to move?'

'It's bigger, for one reason. Another is that it's on the ground floor with a large garden out at the back. The opportunity was there and I took it. And also, I've got a tenant lined up for my old flat, someone who did me a big favour.'

'That's good.'

'Oh, and another thing, the new apartment is suitable for dogs, now I come to think of it.'

'Do you mean Charlie?' said Maria.

'Why not?'

Maria thought about it . . . for ten seconds. 'Are you sure, Luke?'

'D'you think he'd be happy to live with me?'

'Ecstatic,' she said. 'No long car journey to my place, no small flat.'

'And no Maria. For a while at least. So how about it? Shall we go and inspect my property when I've finished my business meeting?'

'You've forgotten the Open Studio Event,' she said.

He looked dumbfounded. 'I have! I can't believe it.'

She smiled. 'You're in a bit of a fix then aren't you?'

'Not if you're there in the studio, standing in for me until I get back. Would you do that, Maria?'

'Of course,' she said.

'Should anyone wish to make a purchase there are red stickers in the desk drawer to indicate that the painting is no longer for sale. They can pay at once or leave a deposit and then pick the painting up when the exhibition closes. OK?'

'OK,' she said. 'But won't they expect to see the artist in person?'

'Most of them won't care. Less embarrassing for them. And those that do . . . well, tell them you're my fiancée and I'll be back soon.'

'But that wouldn't be true.'

His eyes danced at her. 'Do you want me to get down on one knee?'

She looked at the ground at her feet and

pretended to consider it. 'Maybe later?'

'I love you, Maria. Do you know that?'

She felt warm colour in her cheeks. 'Would you trust me with your precious paintings if you didn't?'

'I trusted you with *Dreamcatcher* too.'

She smiled. 'As I would trust you with my life,' she said.

*   *   *

Maria reached into the pocket of her jeans, took out the key that Luke had given her and unlocked the studio door. It felt warm in there and slightly stuffy so she opened two of the windows, then wandered around again looking at the paintings as if she hadn't seen them before.

No-one came in for some time and when at last a young couple wandered in from outside, she was sitting at the desk trying to look efficient. Several other potential customers followed as the afternoon wore on.

She was answering questions about the locality of one of the paintings when she became aware of someone standing behind her, silently waiting.

'I'll take it,' said the man who'd been asking the questions. 'I've been looking for a painting of Leverton Locks.'

Maria tried not to feel flustered as she explained when the painting would be ready for collection, accepted the cheque for the full amount and filled out a receipt. It was a large sum, almost unbelievable. She thought fleetingly of Gary and his comments about the price of the paintings that day in the canal-side pub. Then, turning around, she recognised the girl waiting to speak to her.

'I won't be a moment, Bella,' she said.

'I came to see Luke about the flat,' the other girl said.

'And here he is now,' Maria said, hearing the sound of the outside door opening and footsteps she recognised.

Luke's face broke into a smile. 'So you two girls have met already?'

Bella nodded, looking slightly awkward. She twisted a lock of her dark hair round one finger. 'I'd like us to be friends, Maria,' she said.

'You're a true friend already,' said Luke warmly. 'If it wasn't for you alerting me to some sharp practice by *Club Sonek Enterprises* they would have been the company taking over in the marina and where would Polly and Neil be then?'

Maria took a deep breath. She had wondered about that other company, believing that Luke was connected with them in some way. She hadn't been entirely wrong after all. But she wouldn't tell Polly how close she had been to losing her dream.

'Trick merchants,' Luke said with feeling.

'And Bella had the courage to warn me about their dirty tricks even though it concerned her own brother.'

'I knew it wasn't right,' said Bella.

Maria was silent. Oh yes, that made sense. Pulling out the mooring pegs and almost setting *Dreamcatcher* adrift . . . if they were the culprits.

She smiled at Bella. 'Of course we'll be friends,' she said.

*   *   *

'Plenty of room in my new apartment for the three of us,' said Luke as they walked towards it past the narrowboats lined up at the metal jetties.

'Charlie too?'

'He'll make a good page boy at our wedding, don't you think?' he asked with a grin. 'So what flowers should he carry?'

She laughed shakily. 'Page boys don't carry flowers.'

'This one will,' Luke said firmly. 'Water lilies, don't you think?'

'Those pretty yellow ones,' she said. 'They'll show up well against his black coat.'

She smiled, imagining Charlie's reaction.

Luke was suddenly serious. 'Could you bear the life here with me, Maria?' he asked and then moved swiftly and took her in his arms. 'Today's dream,' he said. 'Tomorrow's reality.'

And she knew without a doubt that this was so.

Chivers Large Print Direct

If you have enjoyed this Large Print book and would like to build up your own collection of Large Print books and have them delivered direct to your door, please contact **Chivers Large Print Direct**.

Chivers Large Print Direct offers you a full service:

✧ **Created to support your local library**

✧ **Delivery direct to your door**

✧ **Easy-to-read type and attractively bound**

✧ **The very best authors**

✧ **Special low prices**

For further details either call Customer Services on 01225 443400 or write to us at

Chivers Large Print Direct
FREEPOST (BA 1686/1)
Bath
BA1 3QZ

ROSEACRE

STANBOROUGH
LODGE

Cole Green House

ROSEACRE

CHURCHFIELD
HOUSE

BARNSIDE